BRICK CITY 2

By Kariem

Copyright ©2016 Luther Garner

BRICKS4Life Publishing
2 Keer Avenue #3
Newark, New Jersey, 07112

Editor, Chyna S.

ISBN:9780692824825
ISBN:0692824820

Library of Congress Control Number:2014950861

Website: www.bricks4lifepublishing.com
Facebook:
www.facebook.com/BRICKS4LifePublishing/home

Manufactured in the United States

Acknowledgments

I thank God for making all things possible!

To all of my Scudder Homes family, our legacy lives on forever!

My supporters of BRICK CITY and BRICK CITY 2, I am dedicated to giving you the best I can. Thank you for all your patience and love.

"Whatever God Does is For the Best!"

To all the staff at Clara Maass Medical Center, you people are awesome.

My Executive Producer / Promoters James Illogik Townsend and Ty of Illuztriouz Entertainment, you two have worked hard on taking these novels to another level, much respect.

David "Indikator" of Enter The Zone TV out in Philly, thanks for the support on your Hip Hop TV show.

Queen Latifah and Roxanne Shante, you ladies support your people, thank you.

Special thanks to Joe A.K.A. Papo-Joe, you have always held me down, I love you.

Mr. Harold "Cadillac" Fairwell, much love, unc.

Teachers are some of the best people in the world, so, Latrise; words cannot explain how proud I am of you. Beautiful, you keep up the great work.

Anitra, we love you.

Darren, let's get our business pumping, son, A.K.A. D. Writer Block.

Tasha and Relly Rell, I love y'all!

Buddy Love, much respect.

Blaame, I got you Dashon. I love my nephew.

Congratulations, Pete!

To all the men and women across America behind the walls, the fight is never over, much love.

To my people's in South Carolina Department of Corrections that keep it one hundred, one love.

Gloria and Carolyn, y'all are always my Brick City ride or die chicks.

Cheryl F. I have some more novels for Long Island, NY. Tell Tina, Danna, and Gwen, hello. Always love.

Sheon, finally part two. Tell my partner, Dianne, hello. Love you, Ms. Jersey.

Chyna S. You made my novel pop off. You are great, much love, my sister, and much respect.

Mia, you help me so much, you are always a blessing, love you.

Handsome Jose and Tate love my family to pieces.

Red, I am so proud of you!

Lulu H, you see your family work, baby!

Lol, Dionne, hey mother!

Shout out to Dorothy. God bless all you do!

Charlie's Angels, you girls are the best, even when y'all quit, LMAO.

Ba, you have some books to sell, love ya, boss.

My other moms, Romella, love you much.

My Aunt Irene, let's go fishing. Love my baby!

Lil-Muhamad, we love you bruh, R.I.P.

Court St. Get your books.

Puddin, you ready? Love ya.

My family, I love you all. It's too many to name. LOL!

Ms. Serena Williams, congratulations do your thing, we love you.

Shout out to the Court St. Crew and the War Boys, you guys go hard in the paint.

Beeyah, I love you for all the love you have shown. You stood up against the Feds for me that morning, my ride or die!

To all my supporters, much love!

Author's Note

To all who are reading my novel, blessings! I write to express pain, love, freedom, awareness, and happiness. My goals are to touch a person's life that is hurting. To change a negative path to a positive; To be a productive part of society and part of a solution. Too many times we fall short of lack of knowledge. Many people today live within a slavery system from back in the sixteen to seventeen-hundredths. Just read "The Making of a Slave" by Willie Lynch, I promise you will see that this vicious cycle must be broken!

BRICK CITY 2 will take you on the ride of your life. See what I have in store, as always I will have you begging for more. This hot page turner won't let you down. This novel is totally fiction. I guarantee you will love it. I love you all!

Thank you,
Kariem

Chapter 1
Four years later

It is late November Newark has gotten snow for the past three days. Many companies forced to close. The sanitation department worked 24-hours a day. For the first two days, people had to abandon their vehicles due to the icy streets. The snow was melting making the streets terrible to drive on.

Mother nature showed up and showed out. University Hospital, Clara Maas Medical Center, Beth Israel, St. James and East Orange Hospital were all almost filled to the max, due to freezing deaths, car accidents, and people seeking shelter.

The media were begging people to stay indoors. PSE&G had the electricity back on after two long days.

If any stores were open, their shelves were empty. NJ Transit even had their snowplows out helping to restore public transportation.

Knowing she wasn't able to drive, Queen decided to stay at the hospital and work, working two double shifts. She was ready to leave when her shift was over. Walking outside to the front of the hospital, she knew she had to shovel the snow away from her car. She noticed a grimy, dirty looking guy coming towards her as she began to remove snow.

"Hello," he greeted.

"Hi," she replied and continued what she was doing.

"Can I help you clean your car, baby?"

"I got it, thank you."

"You think you all that, don't you?"

"No, not at all. I'm just getting off work. I appreciate the offer, but, I'm straight."

"I can't stand bitches that think their shit don't stink!"

"I'ma mace his ass if he comes too close to me." Queen thought.

"Excuse mi, yah aright?" asked the Jamaican stranger that walked up.

Queen hesitated, and then replied, "Yes, I'm okay thanks."

"Oh, ok, so you Mr. Save a hoe?" stated the rude panhandler.

"Mi dun like yuh vibes, step off!" The Jamaican showed the handle of a snub nose 44 Magnum pistol.

The panhandler's eyes looked as though they came out his head. "You good buddy; I was just leaving anyway." The grimy man wasted no time getting away.

"I appreciate that. He was becoming a pain."

"I'm Patrick."

"You dun nuh mi, but mi nuh ya. Yuh, Kaleem's friend, right? Mi hab a clothing store on Grove Street. Take mi card wit mi number. Take it, mi yuh brother now. Call mi yuh need any ting."

"Ok, but I never met or heard Kaleem speak of you before."

"Never mind dem tings, Kaleem's mi good, good friend, much respect to him."

"Ok Patrick, thanks."

Patrick walked to his white Expedition with tinted windows that boasted a green, black, and yellow Jamaican flag. He waited until Queen warmed up her car and pulled off. Queen watched him through her rearview mirror until he turned right on South Orange Avenue going towards Irvington. This made her think about her and Kaleem…

***

"Home sweet home." Queen thought as she pulled up and parked her car. *"Oh boy, I forgot to leave the heat on, it's freezing in this place."* She thought as she walks in her house. *"I'm so tired, those hours are getting to a sister. Kaleem's friend came right on time. When that guy called me a bitch, I should have maced him. That had to be a gun Patrick showed him the way he hauled ass."*

Before undressing and showering, she turned on her slow jams. The sounds of Michael Jackson's "The Lady In My Life" flowed through the speakers. The apartment began to warm up. She went through her mail; bills, bills, and more bills. What's a girl to do, they must be paid.

Queen hoped in the shower; relaxed as the hot water came beating down on her body, penetrating the muscles of her curves. She stepped out the shower, water dripping down her sexy body. *"What a relief!"* She dried off and lit a few candles. As she sat on her bed to lotion up her body, the smell of mint suddenly began to fill the air.

It's been four years since Kaleem has been gone. Queen couldn't stop thinking about the last time she heard his voice. She could still feel his presence as if he had never left, she was still in love with him. Some say she's crazy, but she didn't care, they could think and say what they want.

She began to pray: *Dear God, you know my heart, father. I thank you in advance for all you do, please, look after all my love ones and friends, even the people I don't know. Lead me in the right way to go in life. I ask that the life I give reflect you. Be with the many brothers and sisters that are lost and in prisons across this cruel world, no matter what race they are. Allow your angels to carry me and keep me safe in your mighty name I ask these things...*

***

The next evening

After another long day at work, Queen decided to stop by Pat's house to speak with her. They have not seen each other in months. As she waited for Pat to open the door, she stood there singing to herself, "I've changed" by Jaheim and Keyshia Cole...

"Hi, Queen!" Pat said excitedly when she opened her door.

"Hi, honey, long time, right?"

"Damn right, come on in and sit down, you still look good."

"Thanks, and you're always looking like a teenager, Pat."

"I try my best until I have to beat an old woman's ass." they laughed.

"Girl, I remember the first day we met at the hospital four years ago, Kaleem was drooling over you."

"He was talking slick too."

"Girl, I don't know what you did to him, but you had him open!"

"I fell in love with his heart and mind. I never knew I could love like I have for any man. Once I saw his heart was authentic, it was a wrap. You know we never had sex."

"Girl, you can tell that to somebody else."

"Now, don't get me wrong, I would have loved to tear him up, but, I'm infected with AIDS."

"What!" Pat exclaimed. "Hold the hell up you're telling me you had it all this time?"

"Yes, that is correct."

"C'mon, ain't no way Kaleem knew that shit."

"Aw, yes, I told him and he was upset at first and then after we talked about it. He was stern to the fact that he wanted to be with me. Then the murder happened at my mom's house. You know she saw everything, she was right there. She cared a lot for Kaleem. She thought we would make a good couple. I can hear her telling him now, 'Whatever God Does is For the Best!' he fell in love with her. He would call and check on her. You know he even went to church with me?"

"Girl, I know if he stepped into any church it would have burned down. The last time he went to church was when he was a kid."

"He told me he was tired of the drug game."

"My nephew has a sweetheart he would never start anything, but when it was on. It was on!"

"Woman to woman, Pat, your nephew turns me on so much. I still get wet just thinking about him."

"Shit, girl, all that time, to each its own, you good."

"That night everything happened was agony in my life. It seemed like my whole world shattered right in front of me."

"I recall that day when Jersey City Police pulled you two over and locked Kaleem up, and you were scared as hell."

"For what? I didn't have or know anything. They tried to scare a sister up, but I watch too much Court TV for that." they both laughed. "A lot of these guys need to know they have a right not to tell too."

"Girl, you better check and see if your shit is still down there all those years. Ain't no way I could do that, not even a quickie." they both laughed.

"No, not even a quickie."

"You want some more tea?" Pat asked.

"I'll have one more."

"Every since Omar came into my life I have been happy, girl. He knows I love his bald-headed ass, and I keep him smiling."

"Obviously, he got you sprung I can see it in your eyes."

"Hold on, let me get the phone," Pat told Queen. "Hello,"

"Hi, Ms. Ward."

"What's up, Na'eem?"

"Check this out. First, how are you?"

"I'm good," she replied.

"You know I found out that the state will be bringing the murder to trial soon, and they are going to try and tell Queen and Ms. Inez what they want them to say on the stand. I want to tell them so they can be on point on how they can play dirty. You know the system isn't always fair."

"Yeah, I can imagine why the Lady Justice wears a blindfold. They have everyday citizens as jurors, and uneducated to their dirty tricks. Jurors will convict an innocent person because the prosecutor manipulated their conscious thought pattern to influence a guilty verdict. You know, this year I read about how they lied about DNA of a man, sentenced him to death, and he was, in fact, innocent. To top it off, we the taxpayers pay these people that have taken an oath to stand by the law."

"My sister, you are on point. Now, how about this, when they are caught doing underhanded shit nothing happens to them? So the government can miss me with that equal rights bullshit." Na'eem said angrily.

"By the way, Queen is here now."

"Give me twenty minutes and I'll be over there. I want to make sure they won't be vulnerable to their dirty tricks."

"Ok, see you soon, Na'eem." They hung up their phones.

"Queen, that was one of Kaleem's partners, Na'eem, he is on his way to talk to you."

"Talk to me about what?"

"Relax, he will be over here in a few. How do you deal with all that's on your plate?"

"By the grace of God, girl. I take it one day at a time, stay prayed up, and don't deal with negative people."

"Girl, you are still blessed."

"In fact, I will be a speaker at the Kings and Queens Charter School next month."

"Remind me I'll get Omar to come too."

"Who is it?" Pat yelled after hearing the doorbell ring.

"It's Na'eem!"

"Hey, Na'eem, you got here pretty quick, come in. Queen this is Na'eem."

"Yes, hi, I remember you from the basketball game at Green Acres," Queen told him.

"Yeah, that was me. I wanted to tell you, those prosecutors are going to come at the both of you, threatening you guy, and trying to get you to say what they want you to say, that's how many of them operate. The corruption is about who they want the most not anything about the law or your rights. What rights when they put them in place. We were not even considered all of a man, so unless they are gonna redo them, the laws will never be fair. Keep them envisage, never let them know or think you're not on their side; go along with them. Then, once you get on that stand, expose their ass! Or you can take the fifth amendment, your right to remain silent. Trust me, you won't regret it.

"When is the trial?" Queen asked.

"I hear soon. Just be on point about what's going on. Kaleem is my dude and I'm not letting anyone shit on him just because he is not around."

"Thanks for telling me."

"We have to all show our support in this situation," Pat added.

"Where is Omar?" Na'eem asked.

"He should be on his way." she replied.

"Well, ladies, you both have a good evening. I have some business to handle."

"Ok, I got you," Queen told him.

"You still at the hospital, right?" Na'eem asked.

"Yeah, I'm still there."

"Ok, cool. Talk to y'all later." he stated and then left.

"He has always been family to us," Pat said.

"I see he is a straight to the point type of guy. Well, let me get out of here, Pat, I have to go to work in the morning."

"Queen, I'm sorry about how I first came off when you told me about your sickness. I love you, and I'm here for you if you ever need me." She gave Queen a hug.

***

While driving home, Queen called her mom. "Hi, ma," she spoke when the Bluetooth connected.

"Hi, baby."

"How was your day?"

"I cooked some oxtails, rice, and string beans; they are good too. Are you coming to get some?"

"I'm on my way home right now, ma. How about I come tomorrow? Didn't you want to go to the doctor this week?"

"Yeah, I went. Between my Alzheimer's and my cataracts, I don't know which one is worse. But, I'm still thankful, my child."

"Soon as I get a break from work, let's take a trip to Estill, South Carolina, where you were born."

"Sounds good, but, how are we getting there?"

"I'm going to drive."

"I don't know if I can trust your driving that far, girl."

"Ma, my driving skills is good."

"I know, I'm just joking, Queen."

"I'm home now, I will call you back tomorrow. I love you."

"I love you too as well, okay, bye."

"Bye, ma."

Queen wasn't paying attention to her phone at Pat's house, she looked and seen that she had three messages. She checked her voicemail...

Beep: "Hey, girl, this Cookie, you have to get into the holiday spirit, it's Christmas time. Are we going out?"

Beep: "Queen, this is Tyanna, call me if you want to work overtime this weekend."

Beep: Click...

"I hate when people hang up and don't say nothing. Let me jump in the shower before I go to bed." She hopped in the shower and got comfortable. *"I know that God will not give me more than I can handle. God, you have put so much pressure on me. I fell in love with him, and then you took him away from me. I know I will never understand your ways. Right now, I am angry and have hate inside of me. I guess you wanted me to have AIDS so I wouldn't be loved by a man."*

God speaks, *"Who are you to question me? What have you done to deserve the things I have given to you?"*

"Nothing," Queen responds.

"That is correct, I am all the love you will ever need. You understand that I can do anything?"

"Yes, Father." She laid there and fell asleep.

***

"Work, work, work! But what's a girl to do?" Queen thought after only being at work for four hours.

"Hey, Queen," Tyanna called, "did you get my message last night about this weekend? I need you so I can go to the Smoking Groove party."

"You're always on the go. You better be careful, taking all those days off."

"I need a break from all those days I put in last month."

"I got you," Queen told her.

After making all her rounds, it was time for a sister to get her bounce on. She swiped her I.D card at the time clock and left out of there.

Chapter 2

"It's Friday night, and I'm damn sure going to Brookers."
Ronda boasted to herself. *"Let me call and see if my girls are going."*

Buzz, buzz…

"Hello," Jazz answered.

"Hey, girl,"

"Hey, what are you doing?"

"Girl, getting dressed. You already know, I'm rocking some hot shit; a white one-piece leather jumpsuit and a pair of caramel color Chanel heels. I'ma work this shit, girl!"

"Jazz, tell Ronda to get her talking ass off the phone!" Chyna yelled in the background.

"I hear Chyna talking shit,"

"She heard you, Chyna."

"Call Khayyirrah on three-way while I call Dena," Ronda told Jazz.

"Ok, hold on,"

"Hello, Kha,"

"What, ho?"

"Shut the hell up, while I connect Jazz and Dena in," Ronda stated.

"What's up?" Dena asked.

"Hello," Kha replied.

"Hey y'all thots," Ronda said.

"I hope y'all going to be representing down the hill tonight." Jazz told them.

"Kha, what are you wearing?" asked Dena.

"I brought this fly ass brown and white body hugging cashmere sweater-dress and some black Prada boots. I'ma put a whole roll of tissue in my bag."

"Bitch, why?" Ronda asked.

"Because I will be shitting on them tonight!" they all laughed.

"Dena, what are you wearing?" Kha asked.

"A two-piece,"

"Only your ass could pull that shit off," answered Kha.

"Hey, Jazz, put your phone on speaker, I want Chyna to hear this craziness!"

"Ok, go ahead, talk."

"Y'all know how ole boy DD been trying to cut up in this good stuff all summer right, well, you know he wears them tight jeans showing off his print. I brought him to the crib, and when he took his clothes off and I saw what he was working with, I told him my period just came."

"No, you didn't!" screamed Ronda.

"I bet his face was tight as hell," Kha injected.

"I know that little thing would have given me gas!"

"Is Sonya going tonight?" Jazz asked.

"Girl, every since Sonya got that Liberator, she has been busy using that," Ronda added.

"What the hell is that?" asked Kha.

"Y'all have got to get one; It's a wedge-shaped sex pillow that helps you discover the best angle for him to hit that spot, and give you the best sex experience ever," Dena said.

"I want two of them," said Rhonda.

"Y'all, Chyna poured this sexy ass black mini dress on her body and some red bottom pumps. She is working that outfit, y'all!"

"Oh yeah, what about Dena's ass last week at the sports bar at the airport," Kha said. "Y'all know Jahad and Jamal brought that spot?"

"Yeah, we know, we support our people. Now, back to Dena."

Kha continued. "We all know she can dance, she got this guy on the dance floor working him, and then she stopped dancing and walked away pointing at the wet spot on his pants, showing he done bust off in his pants. I wanted to fall out. He was embarrassed as hell."

"That was crazy!" Chyna replied.

"Girl, that night I took two ecstasy pills; it was on. I just didn't want him."

"If I take two ecstasy pills, I'ma kill a joker in bed!" boasted Kha.

"Guess who I saw at Jersey Gardens," Chyna said.

"Girl, who?" Kha asked, eager to know.

"Baseemah from third world and Rakeema."

"What's up with them? They were cool as hell. We were wild back then." said Ronda.

"What's up with Pat?" Kha asked Jazz.

"Ever since she got with Omar Smiley, she's been the good housewife. Shit, he spoils her, he is a good man, her sons spoils her too, she's straight.

"I miss the projects. We used to have so much fun. What about grinding in the stairways or the elevators?" Dena injected.

"How about kickball in the Morton St. Playground; Tiny and Niecy were sure to kick the balls on the roof," Ronda said.

"And JFK, don't forget." Jazz replied.

"What's up with that chic, Queen?" asked Jazz.

"You know Kaleem was trying to wife her before that stuff jumped off over Jersey City," Kha answered.

"Look y'all ho's, it's damn near ten p.m. We better be rolling out," Chyna told them.

"Oh, shit, right!" Ronda replied.

"I'm not responsible for any of them ho's men leaving home tonight. When they see five divas with the potential to shut shit down, all I can say is keep him at home." Kha added, "Aight, y'all let's meet in front of club Brookers."

The girls ended their phone conversation.

***

"Damn, it never fails, Ronda ass late as always. Even picking up Dena she had enough time to be here." Kha said.

Chyna called Ronda. "Girl, where yo slow ass at? We in front of the club already."

"I'm turning on Evergreen now. I'm driving a car not a jet!"

Click! The phone hung up.

"There she is parking her car," said Chyna.

It's grown and sexy time. Some of the hottest rides you ever peeped!

"It's about time," said Kha.

"I know yo slow ass ain't talking!" Ronda shot back.

Ronda wore the hottest BabyPhat brown suede trench coat; people were hawking it.

"We glad y'all made it," said Jazz.

The beat of the loud sound system was coming through the walls. The five divas checked in their coats. All eyes were on them. The DJ is pumping, Nelly's 'Hot In Herre'. The girls hit the dance floor in no time flat. The guys saw the sexy women and put their best dance moves forward. Wyclef up in the DJ booth talking and checking out the scene. The dance floor was jumping with Stevie Wonder "Always".

"Hi sweetie," said Alamin. A sharp light-skin brother with a beige silk suit, white shirt, and black lizard shoes; looking powerful and admiring and admiring how sexy Chyna was looking.

"Hi," she replied.

"How are you tonight? Can I buy you a drink?"

"I'm sorry, but, I am a package deal."

"What do you mean?"

"It's me and my four girls rolling tonight!"

"That's small for a giant, honey, let's go to the bar so I can order a double for everyone since it's so crowded in here."

Chyna admired how smooth Alamin handled the situation she threw at him.

"Which one's are your girls?"

"Those rolling up on us now." Chyna knew she could brag on her girls, they all were beautiful.

Damn, she wasn't lying; he scanned the girlfriends just moving his lips to say hello, the music was so loud.

Dena was shocked when Anthony Abram of lil Bricks came behind and picked her up. "Put me down."

The rest of the divas moved to see who it was. Three other big guys were with him, Eric Williams, and Josh, all representing "Brick City" in the NBA!

"Hey, Mr. Williams," Ronda spoke.

"What's up, Ronda?"

"We were about to beat some ass in here, y'all lucky." he said.

"I see you still haven't changed from school, man or woman can get it, huh!"

"Chyna, I hear you're getting married," Eric stated.

"Yeah, next year. Every since you traded to Boston, I haven't heard from you."

"Let's have a few drinks and grab something to eat."

"I'm straight. Alamin, this is, Eric, he plays for Boston Celtics.

"Yeah, I know who he is. Congratulations on the win last week, homie."

"Thanks, homie."

"Take care, Eric," Chyna said, and then walked off with, Alamin, leaving Eric speechless.

The rest of the girls continued to party until the break of dawn. They knew the rules, *"we came together, we leave together!"*

Jeffery walked up to make sure the girls were good; he worked security. Surely a ladies man, but family to the divas. He was light, tall, and handsome; some called him, Goldie from the "Mack".

Chyna left Alamin to see if her girls were ready to bounce. "Y'all ready?"

"Yeah," Dena replied, "let's go get Jazz, talking to that dude over there."

The guy Jazz was talking to has had way too many shots of Belvedere. He began cursing at her as the girls were walking up.

"We ready, Jazz," said Chyna.

"I am too," she replied.

"Bitch, who you think…" spat the drunk.

Kha and Dena came swinging their razors over Jazz trying to get to the man.

The feathers came out his goose down coat. That gave him enough time to stagger backward out of the way. Security came on the set pronto.

"What happened?" Jeffery asked.

"They tried to cut me, look at my coat! This bitc…" Slap! Jeffery's hand came across the man's face cutting off his words, knocking him back three steps.

"This my family, you understand me, do we understand each other?" The other three bouncers closed in on their prey.

"Yeah, my bad, it was an old coat anyway."

"C'mon, let me walk you girls to your cars."

Dena pulled out a pack of Newports and lit one up. "Thanks, Jeffery!" all the girls said.

"For what? That's what I am supposed to do. Plus, I didn't want y'all to catch a body."

"He just don't know," said Kha. Then they all left.

Chapter 3

Queen's hours at the hospital were becoming longer and longer, to the point, she would meditate on finding another job. She has a few friends at Clara Mass Medical Center. This is a much smaller hospital, but a more friendly atmosphere. The employees always put their heart and soul into their jobs. People love the staff there.

Queen and Natalie sat in the café speaking about catching the All White sale at Macy's. The television played as they both waited for the Angela Show (talk-show) to come on.

"Here comes that heifer, Stacey." Natalie whispered as they both looked in her direction.

Stacey had a beef with Queen for years, she had a hate for her with a passion. Stacey always chased joy through smoking, drinking, or lesbian experience for five years after getting married just to get back at her woman's lover for leaving her. The results were the image of erotic power and recklessness that spun out of control.

"Queen, you must work this weekend." stated Stacey.

"I'm sorry, Stacey, I made plans already."

"No, sweetie, let me say it this way," If yo ass don't work this weekend, you won't have a job. Now that I broke that down to you, try me!" She put a smirk on her face and walked off throwing her hips with force.

Natalie and Queen spoke to Ena as she came to their table. "I see the wicked bitch of Newark just came by." said Ena.

"You ain't lying, girl, she is a hot mess!" Natalie responded.

"I had to transfer from working with her before I went to jail for beating her ass, and she ain't worth my freedom," Ena added.

Stacey and Queen worked together at the hospital years ago. Things were good between the two until a guy named Shawn took Queen out to lunch. See, Shawn was Stacey's man and Queen had no idea. Stacey confronted her with the issue that he was off limits. Shawn never got any goodies from Queen, but there was no explaining that to Stacey. Ever since that, she despises the ground Queen walks on. She would do anything and everything to make her life a living nightmare. Stacey had left the hospital seven years ago, went to college and became a doctor. Now she is back and is

Queen's supervisor; Queen's life is a constant struggle. Some people get older, but never grow up!

"I can't believe she is still beefing with me! I never had anything against Stacey."

"She does anything to ruin people's joy. She is on a power trip." Ena added.

"I have no reason to compete against her. I have tried to tell her this is nonsense. I don't know how much more I can take before I give her a free pair of shades." Queen said, fed up.

"Why would you give her a free pair of shades?" Natalie asked.

"Because after I drag her ass she's gonna need to cover her black eyes!" the girls laughed together.

"How about the time she had her cousin meet her in the parking lot and tried to jump me; I beat them both with the club that goes on my steering wheel. Then she kept slashing my tires until security saw her on camera, and the job made her pay for them."

Some people will die holding on to grudges and hatred before they forgive. The crazy part is they give people so much energy, thinking negative thoughts. Now Stacey is a very beautiful book smart lady with very little common sense. She is very curvy, one hundred and sixty pounds, and natural black curly hair. She always follows the in-crowd, whatever comes out new, she is chasing. She has a void inside of her that she's been trying to fill for years.

"I'm not putting up with her much longer. I'll just go to another department."

"What if she comes there?" Natalie asked.

"I'll then just find another job, point blank."

"No, honey, you can't leave us, we need you here. You bring happiness around everywhere you go. I don't know why you don't rub off on Stacey!"

"It takes longer with pit bulls," Queen joked.

"Girl, I think she just wanted to become a doctor, hoping you would still be around so she could be the black cloud over your head." Natalie stated.

"Well, she needs to get a life!" Queen shot back. "Hold on, our show is on."

"Welcome to the Community Outreach Show! I'm Angela, your host! We have a great show ahead of us today. Please meet a good friend of mine, Mr. Jose DeValle, a top lawyer out of Hoboken, New Jersey. And to the left of him is Momma Dixon, the mother of all the children from Scudder Homes. (Audience applause) We have you two here today to speak about the school that has been in the spotlight for the last four years. The Charter School for Kings and Queens! Let's start with you, Jose, tell us about the school."

"Thank you for having me on your show, Angela. Well, four years ago I received a phone call from a wealthy man that wanted to give the kids within low-income homes in the Central Ward the same education others kids can afford in life. You see, once a child can broaden their vision, it is a proven fact they will soar in life.

Angela: Is it true, Jose, that the first year you ran into a lot of roadblocks?

Jose: Yes, some higher-ups didn't trust the money for the school was a gift.

Angela: That's how they try to shut things down for something good. Hi, Momma Dixon, how are you?

Momma Dixon: Hi, Angela, you can call me Hilda. Let me say, I love your show. I have always been a fan of yours, now, Wendy my girl too.

Angela: Why thank you, and by the way, I love Wendy too. How did you get the name, Momma Dixon?

Momma Dixon: Because I act like the moms to every kid I come across. I treat them all the same way I treat my own kids. I just love all children. A good friend of mine, Mrs. Walker, she is involved a lot with the kids as well.

Angela: Well, do you work at the school?

Momma Dixon: Yes, thanks to the twenty-five jobs that would only be filled by residents of the Central Ward.

Angela: What about the crime rate in the area?

Momma Dixon: The crime has dropped more than 75% since the school has been up. The Mayor is doing a good job.

Jose: Allow me to interject something, when this project first started, we placed within our budget, money to hire young adults in the area. Guys and girls had a chance to work fixing up abandoned houses in the area. Teaching them trades and paying

17

them minimum wage. Giving them a sense of value and purpose. The finished homes have been featured in the Star Ledger Newspaper also.

Angela: One thing my mother and father told me, and that's to always stand for positive things. "We are our brother's keeper!"

Jose: It's about four million men/women incarcerated in the United States. And the United States only represent 5% of the global population. Statistics estimates that 70% will go back to prison, and bring more pain. 60% of their children will also find themselves incarcerated. We must change this deadly cycle.

Angela: Wow! Do you want to add something?

Momma Dixon: Sure. We all have a part to play… These kids want to be heard, they want to be loved. Once they see that you sincerely care, they tend to listen. We must support our kids. You see how you can find a liquor store on every corner, that's because we allow it! You don't see that in the suburbs.

Angela: You guys have been great, and I have to wrap up the show. I will be donating twenty thousand dollars to your school! (Audience applause). Hold on, hold on! On behalf of my Sorority Sisters, they have made a pledge of twenty thousand dollars as well, so forty thousand dollars will be given!

Momma Dixon: OMG, thank you, thank you!

Jose: That's great, the students will greatly appreciate this.

"Thank you, that completes our show ladies and gentlemen. Tune in tomorrow and as always, we love you all!"

"I think that's one of the best things for Newark. I love anyone who cares about a child's future." Queen stated.

"Yes, it's a beautiful thing," Natalie responded.

Chapter 4

"Hey, dawg, what's good? Congratulations on your new computer store. I'm sorry I missed the grand opening last month." said Bone.

"Congratulations to you and your wife with those two handsome twin boys."

"Thanks, man. I love me some them."

"As a matter of fact, Shaheed and I were talking about you last week."

"About what?" Dawg inquired.

"The time when y'all went down to Tampa and they tried to rob y'all. That was about three years ago, wasn't it?" Bone stated.

"Yeah, you remember that craziness? That was some life threatening stuff."

"Dawg, you're lucky to be alive!"

"Luck ain't have nothing to do with it, we were blessed to make it out of that alive."

"You know that shit went down with Kaleem and that cop goes to trial this year." Bone stated.

"Word. Kaleem just looked out for the wrong people. He used to tell me, 'let them play themselves like a cheap trick, 'cause dirty slime ball jokers will never make it no place, 'cause they don't want nothing!' That's real talk. I don't see how a guy could put his family on the front line over some shit he did." Dawg added.

"Let me tell you how that shit went down in Tampa– The whole week I didn't feel right. Our driver had an accident with the stash car the same week of the trip. Jungle had just bought a brand new Range Rover, chrome wheels, sports package, all wheel drive, rear high beam lights, X-Box system, wifi hookup, tinted windows with a stash box. Let me tell ya, son, those are some nice trucks. So he took his man Day, he had mad crazy driving skills. I was cool with that, so, me and Shaheed was riding with them to go make our play, feel me? Now, I had my connect for two years and we been doing good business. See he had got killed in Colombia (the country) and his brother Sammy that was still in America tried to take over. Oh, before I forget, the plug which is the connect got hooked up with Sucriss sister Delfene, but the few times we saw each other we didn't speak. I was cool with us not letting them know we knew each other. We arrived at five in the evening. After grabbing a room at the Holiday Inn, everyone wanted to grab something to eat. So we rode to a mom's and pop's soul food joint named, Pearl's. The weather was wet and gloomy. Hearing the rain beat on all that it hit, played so many different tunes to your ears. A girl stood outside trying to stay dry, we all kept it moving inside. Day went back outside and invited the stranger in to get something to eat. She was glad he did."

"What's your name, beautiful?" At one point, you could tell she used to be pretty, but the streets don't discriminate.

"Damn, you working and can't get out the rain?" Jungle stated.

"I had a room, but my John beat and robbed me, and then put me out."

"Don't you think it may be time to give up your job?" Day asked.

"When your father suffered from drug addiction and my mother abused me, sex was a way out for me to forget about the emotional trauma of my childhood. The rush of anticipation and excitement, keep me high enough, you forget about my real life problems. I didn't so much want to deal with it."

"You hold the power even in your weakness! You got to want it more than anybody. I can tell you were a head turner and if you start to love yourself again, you will build yourself back up." Day told her.

"It's a rehab in Richmond, Virgina by my aunt's house, I wanted to try my luck out there." she expressed.

"Tammy, eat your food. I'ma pay for your bus ticket through my phone now. If you want to get help, you will make it. Here is four hundred you can go get high or you can change your life." Day cut through Tammy like a knife. She started crying and couldn't believe a stranger would give her anything without wanting some head or coochie.

"Thank you, all I can say is, thank you!"

"Good luck." All the guys hugged her and bounced.

"I got the phone call, it was Hector's brother, Sammy, asking what's the count... I told him, five."

"That's a lot of cash." Bone said.

"Frankly, Bone, Jungle, and Day saved our lives! You know that family is trained to go. Delfene never answered the door— Hold on, let me backup— Jungle vibe was as though he was a Navy Seal. He told Day to drive past the home about a hundred yards and then turn around. Day noticed that it was too many lights off in a big house like that. He opened up the stash box allowing Jungle to grab his black M-4 with a night vision scope, a two hundred round clip, and an infrared beam; hitting your target would be no problem. Jungle jumped out and blended into the darkness as we pulled in front of the house. Shaheed and I walked to the front door. Shaheed had the duffle bag with the money. The front door was cracked, but I still rang the doorbell. After a brief moment, Delfene opened the door halfway. Sammy stood in the hallway waving us to hurry in. Delfenes eyes stuck on the front door letting us know someone was behind it. I pushed the door hard, catching the man behind the door off guard. His gun blasted off two rounds, one in the floor, and the other the wall. Delfene screamed, running out the house, and we turned to run. The truck was too far to make it to, so we ran to the left trying to find cover behind some cars. The gunshots continued ringing at us. Shaheed had been shot in the leg. The four gunmen were closing in. The sounds of drums beating caught our attention. Jungle began letting his bullets rain out of his M-4; walking into the men shooting, they tried to stand their ground but seen they were no match for Jungle. They tried to run, but Jungle dropped every one of them. He came through like Wu-Tang Clan. Day drove the truck across the lawn right up to us. Everyone jumped in the truck. Yo, we dropped Shaheed and Delfene off at the hospital and she told the detectives some Cuban's had come to the house trying to rob them. She kept it Scudder Homes, giving us time to bounce. So we hit her off with some cash and never been back. That's why I chilled out and opened this store."

"Damn bruh, that was off the meter. Yo, I'ma bust at you later, I got to get to the house." Bone said.

"Ok, that's what's up," Dawg replied.

Chapter 5

Show love, you never know how or when it will come back to you. But, now everybody is not for you, only what they can get out of you… Cheap tricks!

"It ain't my time yet! The ones that want to see them bury me in the ground or some jail cell. I'm standing strong!" Kaleem thought. The sounds of gunshots played over and over inside Kaleem's brain.

"Prayer works," the little voice inside his conscious said.

"Damn, I didn't expect for Inez to find the gun inside the clock with the money and come blasting! She held the gun with two hands and without any hesitation, shot Robo Cop twice in his face opening two large holes on the right side of his face. Forcing the blood to splatter from his brain onto the white walls of her kitchen. Shit was real! As she untied me, she was calm and said. 'Whatever God Does is For the Best!' No doubt because I was 'bout to die!"

"I told you, we should have killed that cop. All that trouble he caused." Mr. Devil said.

"Man, you're just like his ass. All you want to do is rob, steal, and destroy my life, and then bury me!" Kaleem told him.

"I mean, you act like I don't help you! I'ma get at you later before you piss me off!"

"Good haul ass!"

"I'm the one who saved your life. I have plans for your life. Now that I have your attention, I will give you the joy that you can only find in me, IM Your GOD! the Spirit said to Kaleem.

"So, you mean to tell me, it was your plan to have me behind these walls having moms bust her ass just to feed her kids, not knowing how it feels to go shopping for school clothes, waiting on a welfare check, and if your lucky, it may pay the rent; living in an abusive household, not knowing how it was to take a dollar to school to get a snack! Wanting more and getting less!"

"It is some evil people in the world. That's a fact, but I have something for them, now that's a fact. Love yourself, and you will see what I mean.

Kaleem had been locked down for four years. He only gets visits from his lawyer. He knew not to torture himself by expecting people to come see him, knowing it hurts the most when you depend on someone and they let you down! He never mentions Queen. He knew they would use anyone to get a conviction. A white cop being murdered by a black man!

Looking at the four walls, the steel toilet, and sink; the window is as big as your fist and long as your arm, only to see a cement wall. They try to run you crazy if your mind is weak. He is in tune with his mental, no room for defeat. Queen really had his heart, even with AIDs. Wow, what a blind love, got to be from above.

Kaleem picked up the Bible, it seemed like it was talking to him. He looked at the Koran, and it did the same. *"I see both can be a way of life."* he thought. *"I don't know how this road will end, but I got to roll with it because ain't no way I'ma say she did it. She saved my life, pushing Robo Cop's wig back.*

"Ward!" yelled the correction officer. "Lawyer visit!"

***

"Hi, Kaleem," said Devalle. "We got court next month. Just know all they want is a conviction. Trust the firm's fighting for you. I'ma man of my word."

"So, it's next month?"

"Yes, on the tenth. We have Sandy Staford, she is the lead prosecutor on your case, and she is a real bitch. Ain't no telling what type of stuff she will try. We can try to plead out, but you said trial. They have about twenty witnesses, and fifteen is incarcerated.

"Incarcerated! What're their names?"

"I will send that to you. I'm not worried about them. They're only looking for a deal to cut their sentence. I do know the old lady and her daughter, and an autopsy doctor will testify."

"So, some prosecutor bitch that doesn't know me will get up in front of twelve Jurors and talk about me like a dog and take me away from my family for life. Not concerned about the circumstances, only a conviction! It's going to be a war inside that courtroom."

"Have you been in contact with, Inez or Queen?" the lawyer asked.

"No, not at all."

"You need me to take care of anything?" DeValle asked.

"As a matter of fact, yes. I want you to open the eyes of twelve Jurors. Jurors don't know that the authorities want to keep them confined and manipulate their conscious thought pattern to influence a guilty verdict. So they need to be mentally awakened. How at times, some prosecutors, solicitors, and judges abuse their position to compromise a conviction? Just because they are held to the highest standards of good character. They took an oath to stand on the law. And the taxpayers pay their salaries. The kicker is when they have been caught doing illegal activities such as falsifying evidence, witness tampering, wrongful conviction, lying, and killing through death sentences only to find out it was the wrong person. These people are above the law until they are held responsible for their actions. How can you trust them? Our government knows this goes on across the United States but have yet to put a stop to this madness! Having your life in the hands of someone who don't care about you or know your struggle. Don't get me wrong, prison is needed…"

"Kaleem, trust me, I know just what you mean. I've been doing this for a while and it's nowhere near fair play! Well, I'm going to do some work. Take care. Oh, I'll have you some clothes for trial. Talk to you later."

"Thanks for coming." Kaleem waited on the CO to come take him back to his cell.

***

Mr. DeValle really was doing his best to bring Kaleem home. He stopped by Diamondz N Da Ruff café & lounge to grab some good food downtown. To his surprise, Shaq was there. He would be having a three on three tournament and buying five hundred kids sneakers and free tickets to the movies.

Sandy the prosecutor happened to recognize Mr. DeValle. "Hello, Jose."

"Hi, Sandy." he replied.

"You know, Jose, I just thought about how in the hell you could represent someone like that!"

"Well, for the record, sweetie, that's my job and it's how I feed my family!"

"I hope you got paid because we are going to fry and burn his ass. Ain't no way he will be back on the streets. He killed a good cop."

"You know, Sandy, you and any other that lie, cheat, and steal people's lives just to make a name for themselves are evil. And you're a low-class hooker, you do anyone, anywhere to get what you want."

"Oh, baby, you want me to give you some?"

"No thank you! Listen, lady, I took an oath and have always been loyal to that, unlike yourself. Now, please, let me eat in peace."

"Fine, but remember what I told you. Goodbye." She removed herself from the table.

Kaleem knew that so many weak, wannabe men bitched up and made record deals; What the hell could he expect out of Queen or her moms. It's bad enough with the illegal things that are done to lock people up, and then they convince people to say what they want them to say on the stand in court to secure a conviction.

Chapter 6

Trial time! No trial has been this big since the Organized Crime Drug Enforcement, Task Force, DEA, FBI, IRS, and BON plotted together in 89 and broke any law they had to and got Akbar off the streets. Akbar is well loved for never sucking off the government or play their dirty games. His daughter fought it out with her pops to the end, that's how to love.

The Sheriff Department beefed up their security today, due to Kaleem's high profile trial. Rumor has it that some officers have deviated from what they were hired to do in order to devour Kaleem. The courthouse is like Fort Knox. Traffic backed up everywhere; West Market, Martin Luther King Blvd., Springfield Ave. Howard St., Court, West Kenny, and University Avenue; people walked for blocks. Kaleem was well loved, so Brick City came big!

The mahogany wood in the courthouse shined enough to see your face in it. The thick stained glass windows blocked the sun's rays from the 95° weather. People stood in line for over an hour to see how the justice system would play out today. The enormous crowd of supporters took up all standing space available. Mr. DeValle asked that the witnesses be secluded, this way no one could hear what the others testified to. Mr. DeValle came out the bathroom praying: this was a must before every single case.

"Hi, Jose." spoke the bailiff.

"Hi, Mike, how is everything? I need to see my client before the trial starts."

"Jose, between you and me, let his ass burn!"

Mr. DeValle gave him a harsh look through the gates.

"Hi, Kaleem."

"Hi, Mr, DeValle. Do you know they want me to wear some type of shock bet!"

"No way! I'll be right back."

Knock, knock, knock.

"Yes!" said the Judge inside his chamber.

"Your Honor, it was brought to my attention that the Sheriff Department wants my client to wear a shock belt. My client has no violent record or escape charges, and this would violate his rights greatly!"

"Well, I have to agree with you, that will bring him undone hardship. For the protection of his rights, I will not allow him to wear it. I'll call down there, now."

"Thank you, Your Honor."

"Now this trial will start on time!" the Judge stated.

"Sure, I'm ready."

"Good!"

"Kaleem, get dressed, without the shock belt."

"That was fast!"

"Judge Axelrod is a fair man. That's a good thing for our side. It's packed out there, Kaleem, I need you to listen carefully. It will be a pad and pen in front of you; I need you to write down anything you think I need to know."

"Is Queen and Inez out there?" asked Kaleem.

"I'm sure they are. You look good in black, the suit fits you well. Did you pray?"

"Thanks. Of course, that's a must!"

"Kaleem, no matter what happens, know I gave you 110%."

"That's all I could ask for."

"Let's go and grab our seats. This is where the rubber meets the road." the attorney said.

Both men entered the courtroom. People began greeting Kaleem, making him aware of their support. He couldn't recall all their names but can recall all their faces. The officers in there were tensed, and ready for some action.

"All stand!" said the bailiff. "The Honorable Judge Axelrod presides!"

"Thank you. Take your seats, please." the Judge spoke and then said. "Good morning, I am here today to make sure both sides follow the laws in which our government sets forth. To the Jury, this is a great task you have ahead of you today. I ask that you don't discuss any of this case with anyone. The defendant does not have to prove one single thing he is innocent. The state must prove beyond a reasonable doubt that this man is guilty as charged and the charge is murder! I will not tolerate any outburst or commotion during this trial. So please keep your composure! If not I will have to throw you out or you will be fined."

At the moment you can hear a pin drop. Everyone's eyes looked towards a woman with a black briefcase, glasses, and a long white Gucci dress, making her way to sit down next to Kaleem and Mr. DeValle. "Hi, guys," she whispered. "Mr. DeValle, if you don't mind, I'm here to help Kaleem." She extended her hand to Kaleem. "I'm Ms. Motto, you can call me, Marie."

"Excuse me," said the Judge, "can we get started now?"

"Yes, I apologize, Your Honor. I would like to put on record, Ms. Motto will be assisting me with this case."

"Fine, please stand and state your name for the record." the Judge told her.

"Hi, Judge Axelrod, I'm Marie Motto and my firm will be assisting Mr. DeValle representing, Mr. Ward today."

"Well, Ms. Motto, it is surely a pleasure to have you in my courtroom today. You have been busy lately."

"Oh, shit!" thought Staford. Then came a perplexed look on her face.

"Work like always, Your Honor."

"Ok, we will have an opening statement from the State first. Ms. Staford, the floor is yours."

Kaleem sat at attention after scanning the courtroom with people he hasn't seen for years.

Ms. Staford got out her seat and began to state her case. "Good morning ladies and gentlemen. I thank you for being here. We all would rather be somewhere else today, but unfortunately, we are here. The State of New Jersey and the many people that pay taxes want justice. Mr. Wells and I will prove, that man," she pointed a finger towards Kaleem, "murdered, in cold blood with no remorse, killed a police officer that has been serving your community for fourteen years. This man was happily married with two kids. This man needs to be off our streets forever! He doesn't care about the law at all!"

Kaleem, Mr. DeValle, and Ms. Motto were all writing down notes. Kaleem slides his note to Mr. DeVlle: *"That bitch!"* Mr. DeValle waved a hand to Kaleem as to tell him to keep calm.

Ms. Staford continued, "Please, listen to my partner, Mr. Wells."

"Morning folks. My partner, Ms. Staford was nice. I'm not nice nor do I come to be nice. I am here to put Mr. Ward behind bars for life! I have witnesses, evidence, and a dead cop!" Mr. Wells walked over to the Jury box and looked over at Kaleem. "I don't see how anyone would represent somebody like that!"

"I object, Your Honor!" Mr. DeValle stood up angrily.

"Sustained! Mr. Wells, please stay within the rules of the court. The jury, please, disregard the last statement from Mr. Wells. The defendant has every right to be represented by counsel."

"Yes, Your Honor." the Attorney stated, and then continued. "Juror, Mr. Roy Scott is dead, and he can't tell you who killed him. You will have to speak for him and his family today."

"Objection, Your Honor!" yelled Ms. Motto.

"This is my last warning, counsel! Jurors, please, once again, disregard his last statement."

"Allow me to call my first witness, pathologist, Dr. Zen."

The court registrar swore Dr. Zen in and he took the stand.

"Dr. Zen, would you please tell the Jury the condition Mr. Scott's body was in."

"Sure. Mr. Scott had been shot twice with a .40 caliber's bullets, that entered the right side of his face and exited on the left."

"Dr. Zen, did that cause Mr. Scott's demise?"

"That will be correct, sir."

"Thank you, I have no more questions. Please answer any question the defense may have for you."

Mr. DeValle began his questioning. "Dr. Zen, how are you today?"

"I'm well, thanks."

"Dr. Zen, was officer Scott under the influence of any drugs or alcohol?"

"No, not to my knowledge."

"Well, let me put my question like this; did you send his blood out for a DNA sample to be tested?"

"No, I did not."

"Well, is it safe to say, you dropped the ball?"

"Huh!"

"The hospital autopsy report shows that Officer Scott had a substantial amount of cocaine and alcohol in his system."

"I didn't test it, so I won't comment on that."

"Thank you, Dr. Zen. I have no further questions." Mr. DeValle knew he won that round with the Jury.

The next witness called to the stand was, Billy Black. He was sworn in and took the stand.

"Mr. Black, can you tell the Jury how you know Mr. Ward and what he told you?" Sandy Staford asked.

"Sure. Check it. I was in my jail cell when he came in from the county jail. He told me he killed a cop. He said the cop was trying to kill him and he wasn't going to jail and he shot him five times all over his body."

"Thank you, please answer all the questions defense have for you."

"Mr. Black, why would Mr. Ward tell you something like that?" DeValle asked.

"Jail talk, stupid, I don't know!"

"Can you please tell the Jury how you got your two arm robbery charges dropped, without ever going to court?"

"Huh?" he responded in shock.

"Tell them how your charges disappeared!"

"I don't know, why are you asking me? I guess they lost the paperwork!"

"No more questions, you may step down."

***

This is the seventh day of the trial with only a few witnesses left, and the courtroom is still packed. They called Director, Mr. Baye to the stand.

"Mr. Baye, how long Mr. Scott has been on the force?" Ms. Staford asked.

"Fourteen years."

"Isn't it true that Mr. Scott put a lot of criminals behind bars, helping to protect the people of Newark?"

"Yes, that's true!"

"Thank you, no more questions, Your Honor!"

"Your Honor, I have a few questions for, Mr. Baye!" Ms. Motto stood and said. She stood at five feet five, looking like a beautiful Italian supermodel. All eyes were on her when she stood. She unbuttoned her blazer revealing her white blouse that went well with her blue Kenneth Cole mini skirt. She demanded attention in this outfit!

"Director Baye, how long have you been on the force?" she inquired.

"Twenty-five years, I'm proud to say!"

"Can you tell us what the Internal Affairs department does?"

"Sure! They investigate any complaint that comes from within the force or from citizens which we protect and serve. They make sure we abide by the law and don't fall to corruption."

"Now, can you tell us what concerns Internal Affairs had with Mr. Scott?"

"Objection, Your Honor!" Staford jumps out her seat. "Mr. Baye can't testify to hearsay!" she boasted.

"That's right!" injected Mr. Wells.

"I understand that, Your Honor. This is why I would like to submit this exhibit as evidence. Here is one for you and the State as well." Ms. Motto worked the runway of the court as she exposed the paperwork.

"Ok, you may continue, Ms. Motto. The objection is overruled!" the Judge stated.

"Thank you, Your Honor." she continued, "Mr. Baye, can you tell the Jury what you have in your hand?"

"I have a printout from Internal Affairs, with a list of allegations concerning Officer Scott."

"Please, read them."

"**Sure assaults:** *Shaking down drug dealers, Obstruction of Justice, abuse of power, entrusted power for private gain, and stealing.*"

Damn! Some of the crowd whispered amongst each other. Many others shaking their heads. Even the Judge had to adjust his glasses while reading along with, Mr. Baye. Ms. Motto knew she had hit a home run!

"I don't have any more questions. Thank you, Mr. Baye!" she looked over at Sandy's table with a penetrating smile.

Ms. Staford knew Ms. Motto was one of *the* best attorneys in the county. It would be insane to think otherwise! Mr. Wells knew he had to fire back and fast. His hole card would be Queen and her mother.

"Your Honor, our next witness is, Queen Mack!" the bailiff opened the side door allowing Queen's entrance into the courtroom.

"I know that bitch ain't going to testify for the State." said Ronda.

"There goes the dirty bullshit," Dawg said to Hakim.

Both Kaleem and Queen's eyes locked within each other. Kaleem softly and smoothly moved his lips saying *"I love you!"* Her eyes fell stuck in a daze, on the man she wanted so much.

"Hello, can you state your name for the court, please?" asked Mr. Wells.

"Yes, Queen Mack!"

"Can you tell us, how you know Kaleem Ward?"

A long pause reserved the silence of the entire court.

Mr. Wells had to resuscitate Queen back to earth. "Ms. Mack, can you answer the question, please!"

"At this time, I would like to obtain my Fifth Amendment Right, to remain silent. I don't even want to be here today!"

"Ms. Mack, has anyone threatened you in any way?"

"Yes!"

"Please, please, give us their names so they can be dealt with!" said Mr. DeValle.

"The prosecutor's office told me, I had to come or they would issue a warrant for my arrest!"

"So, you're telling me, you won't be answering any questions today?"

"That is correct!" she replied.

"You may step down." the Judge stated.

She stepped down and forced her way to find a seat behind Kaleem.

"I thought you said we had her on our side." Mr. Wells said to Ms. Staford.

"I don't understand myself." she replied.

Mr. Wells pulled himself together, wiped the sweat from his forehead and called his last witness to the stand. "Your Honor, we would like Ms. Inez Mack to take the stand, please."

Ms. Staford took over. "Hello, Ms. Inez."

"Hello." she spoke in a soft voice.

"Can you please tell us, is it true that Mr, Scott was murdered in your apartment?"

"Yes, that is true."

"Is it true that Kaleem Ward was at your apartment during this same time?"

"Yes, that is true also."

Staford was feeling good with this witness. Thinking she has the Jurors in her favor, finally. "Can you tell us how many gunshots were fired that evening?"

"I recall it being two shots!"

"*Damn!*" Kaleem thought to himself. "*I know she not gonna tell what really happened that night. I'm taking the charge for her!*"

Sandy's strategy was to let the defense bring out the million dollar prize to the Jury that Kaleem killed Officer Roy Scott (Robo Cop).

"Thank you, Ms. Inez Mack, for doing your part as a law abiding citizen. Please answer any questions the defense may have at this moment."

"Hi, Ms. Inez. My name is, Ms. Motto. Can you please, tell me why Mr. Scott was at your home?"

"Hello, he told me that, Kaleem was meeting him there. When Kaleem got there, Mr. Scott pulled his gun out on him!"

"What happened next?"

"They demanded money from Kaleem."

"Did you... No, let me rephrase my question... When you say, 'demanded money', who are you talking about?" Ms. Motto wanted to know. She asked plainly.

Inez took a drink of water, she looked at the prosecutors, and then to the Jurors. She never looked towards Kaleem. She said to herself, "*Whatever God Does is For the Best!*"

"Can you answer the question?" Judge Axelrod demanded.

"I was talking about the other officer that was with Mr. Scott!"

"Excuse me, what did you say?"

"I said, another officer was at my apartment also at the same time Officer Scott was."

"Ok, so let me ask you this, what did this officer do?"

"The officer shot Officer Scott in the face, took the money that was in a shopping bag, and left!"

The crowded courtroom of attendance became loud. No one could believe what they just heard. The mouths of many were left open in shock!

"Order in the court, order!" the Judge insisted, slamming his mallet.

"Your Honor, I'm asking for a direct verdict, that you rule on this case." Mr. DeValle injected.

"All council members come to the bench, now!" The Judge was furious. "What is going on, you mean to tell me, no one knew about this?"

Every counsel face looked as though they had seen Freddy Krueger!

"Ms. Inez, Is this your first time telling anyone this?"

"Yes, Your Honor. Only because the detectives put my statement the way they wanted. Kaleem didn't kill him, the other guy with the badge did!"

"Order, order!" the courtroom erupted with noise again.

"You can step down, please."

Inez made her way down to Queen, who was crying, trying to help her mother sit down. Kaleem sat there stung about what just happened.

"I'm going to let the Jury decide this case!"

"But, Your Honor, you heard what she said. The State has no evidence to prove otherwise!" said Ms. Motto.

"Well State, do you?" asked Judge Axelrod.

"Huh, um, no, only what we have already brought out," Sandy said sadly.

"All attorney's and defendant, please stand to your feet!" the Judge ordered. "Ladies and gentlemen of the court, we have come to the end of this trial. I thank all of you for your time and input."

Kaleem's heartbeat was racing fast. He felt about seven or eight hands touch his body, sending an electric wave of current up and down it. The people were praying, for him, of course. Queen and Inez's hands were among them.

The Judge continued. "It is my job to stand only on the facts of the law on how I may personally feel. It's sad anytime a life is lost in such a matter due to violence. A conviction acquired through the knowing used perjured testimony and allowed to pass uncorrected is unacceptable. Ms. Inez was the State's key witness and her statement was crucial. She testified under oath, that Mr. Ward was not the shooter who killed Officer Scott, and that someone else killed him. The State did not identify the perpetrator. Mr. Ward, I find you, Not Guilty!"

Both sides of the room became unruly and loud for the next fifteen minutes, The crowd chanted as they left out… "Not Guilty, Not Guilty, Not Guilty!

The light of Victory has come. Kaleem's eyes filled with water enough to flow out his eyes as he hugged Inez and Queen. Ms. Inez softly spoke in Kaleems ear, "Whatever God Does is For the Best!"

He repeated, "Whatever God Does is For the Best!"

They took Kaleem back to the county to be processed out.

"Ms. Motto," said Mr. DeValle. "I owe you big time."

"For the record, I took this personally. Staford was talking about me to some of her friends and it got back to me. She can't hold a candle to me, I'm good at what I do." she bragged.

"You surely are, and by the way, that outfit killed the runway!" He flirted.

"Oh, this little thing. I wanted to wear it before gaining any more weight," she said playfully.

"I'll see y'all soon."

The bailiff walked Kaleem into the back.

"Ma, you never told me that's what happened."

"And you never asked, my daughter."

"Let's get out of here! I'm sure these people don't like what just happened."

Everyone was texting, calling, and spreading the news on all social media sites.

Special letter: One Victory does nothing for the lives and freedom of the many men and women who has been kidnapped due to railroading through racial prejudice. Framing by Law Enforcement, false confession, or misconduct. For the many people that DNA Exonerations have saved and cleared your name. That nightmare will live inside forever!

Chapter 7

The county jail received the news that Kaleem had won the trial. Many officers saw Kaleem as their adversary. The news teams and about one hundred spectators filled the lobby outside near the stairway. Mr. DeValle had been waiting for his client so that they didn't drag their feet on doing their job.

"You'll be back if you're lucky!" whispered an officer.

Kaleem didn't respond. Sometimes the best answer is a quiet nothing. Kaleem kept it moving out the sliding doors that separated him from the outside world of people waiting to see him. Walking into the T.V crews, bright lights, and cameras, he looked for Queen. Spotting her with her mother, his partners surrounded them for protection.

Queen embraced her love with a tight hug, softly telling him, he is the love of her life. Caressing her face with the palm of his hands, he directed her lips in front of his and begun to passionately kiss her. Queen had to get a grip, her body fluids began to bubble. She knew the heat within her body had reached its composure. "Welcome home, baby." She pushed back.

"Thank you for standing your ground."

"That's what I was supposed to do. I'm down with you!"

"It can be one hell of a ride."

"I'm one hell of a woman."

"That you are, that you are."

"Ms. Inez," Kaleem spoke.

"Sssh, sssh, some things are better off left alone. Whatever God Does is For the Best!"

"That's for sure! I will come by to see you once I handle a few things." he told her.

"Ok, let me write down my number for you."

Kaleem began shaking hands and hugging people.

"We got three of the same trucks parked side by side, Kaleem, when you are ready, get in the first one in the back seat, slide out to the other side into the middle truck so that nobody follows us," Hakim stated.

"That's cool," Kaleem replied.

"Welcome home star. You mi dude. What the hell is going on with ya?" asked Jamaican Patrick.

"I love you man, how you been?" Kaleem stated and asked.

"Good! Mi put together a big party fa yuh, I mean big."

"I can't be in the front line like that right now, they will be out to kill ya boy!"

"Don't worry yourself, star. When God ready for ya, nothing you can do! Mi takes care of security dem things. Mi calls ya soon."

"When you talking about doing this?"

"About two months or so, I got to call mi boy Strachie in Jamaica and tell him to come too!"

"Patrick is on point with security and I will have some just to make sure." Kaleem input.

"Kaleem, here is a phone for you to have, it's brand new. I picked it up on the way here." said Na'eem.

"Always thinking. Thanks, Na'eem." Right away, he locked everyone's number in his phone and sent Queen a text: *Ready for daddy.*

She texts back: *Wet n ready* ☺ ☺.

He had to look at her face after that text to see her smiling in pleasure.

Kaleem dialed the Lost Boys Myrtle Beach Chapter Motorcycle Club. "Hello," the voice of a big southern man echoed through the phone, named Jodi.

"Yeah, this Kaleem. I need some help."

"What's up?"

"This the deal, I'm having a big party up here and you already know I'ma need some security. I need you to ride up here with your club and I will have a few more clubs at the event also."

"How big?" Jodi asked.

"About three, four thousand out the night."

"Damn, we ain't gonna miss that! Just email me the when and where you can count us in!"

"Cool, I'll talk to you later.

Patrick called to Jamaica. "Yo, Strachie, ya boy Kaleem out of jail."

"Him home? Stop ya lying."

"Real talk star. We need him a big party up here and I want you to bring the island party to help turn it up!"

"That's mi boy, say no more. Jamaica will be repping in full effect in Jersey! Let me know everything."

"Cool." The men hung up the line.

The party will be in two months and there is no time for procrastinating.

Kaleem refused to talk to the news teams. The men walked over to the three trucks that look the same. Kaleem got in the back seat and into the next truck as Na'eem and Hakim got in. All the trucks followed suit as they drove off and split up downtown going in different directions.

Kaleem needed a fresh haircut, so Hakim drives up to All That Cuts Barbershop on Springfield Ave and Twentieth St...

***

"What's good?" Kaleem and Hakim spoke as they walked into the Barbershop. Thick bulletproof glass, two pool tables, two free-throw machines, laptop station for kids to do homework, three 60" 4k T.V's, and solid wood furniture. With about fifteen customers and five barbers, it wouldn't take long at all.

"Yo, what's up, Kaleem!" a few people he knew spoke.

"Oh, shit, welcome home kid. All that shit is on the news." said Dave.

"That's peace fellows, thanks." The shop jumped into their conversation.

"My point is that in this life, blacks in America will never be treated fairly in all aspects of life! And one black president is like a marble on a beach." Malik said.

Mookie the mailman injected. "White America has too much power. They will attempt to brainwash you. We won't have equal rights until they change the laws and sick thinking, then maybe!"

"Yo, check this out," Londell said, "I saw on YouTube, a white guy down in Texas had just robbed a store. Three white cops came up, drew their guns at the suspect, and demanded he drops his gun. He told them to drop their guns. The exchange went on three times and finally, he dropped his gun. Now, you talk about profiling! Now, let that had a been a black guy!"

Everyone in the shop agreed!

"Every since I was in the service I dealt with a lot of racism." said Dave. "But check this, no matter black or white, being racist is plain stupid! Do anyone know who Edward Snowden is?"

"That's that white guy, he's a former contractor for the CIA, who leaked that the government was spying on everyone through internet and phone surveillance," Kaleem answered.

"That's right. How about Gary Webb? No one knew that he exposed the FBI and CIA. Let me add, Mr. Webb is white also! He was a damn good journalist that stood on truth. He told that the CIA was selling drugs in Los Angeles to support the Reagan Administration in efforts to overthrow the Government of Nicaragua. That makes him a hero to me. And a friend of mine told me about Joan Mulholland, a freedom fighter that went through hell fighting for a cause for people of color. And she is still helping society as a librarian, another hero, a civil rights activist, which happens to be Caucasian. We have another white woman, Lynne Stewart, an attorney and human rights activist, known for representing the poor and oppressed. She was convicted in New York on five counts of conspiracy to aid and abet and providing material to support terrorism. But, really, her crime was helping blacks and doing her damn job! That's how the government design things."

Kaleem added. "We all know a system based on punishment and isolation breeds anger and then the difficulty in functioning upon the return to society. The government will lock up any organization that wants to abolish the structure of the government!"

"Little man, what grade are you in?" asked Malik.

"Eighth," JoJo replied.

"Does your school teach Black History?"

"American History."

"But not Black History, correct?"

"Yes, sir. But my grandpa enlightens me on a lot of history. He says, 'there is no mystery when you know your history!'"

"Who is your grandpa?"

"Kariem."

"Ok, what else did your grandpa tell you?"

"That I should never waste energy blaming other people for anything. How the government has a worldwide of manipulation of our history, and since they control the image and information of the past, they will control the future, and they want us to stay illiterate."

"Damn, JoJo, you're an intelligent young man. Like grandpa told you, read and keep reading." Hakim told him.

Someone, please show me The Land of The Free!

"JoJo, God has great plans for your life. I'm sure, never stop absorbing knowledge." said Kaleem.

"All that sound good, but none of that shit putting food on the table." Stated J-Money, a nineteen-year-old gangbanger. "See, me and my set, we look out for each other. Ain't nobody gonna stop me. I do me!"

"How about the people who loves you, what about them?"

"What about them? I take care of myself!" This kid was feisty.

"So you got your own place, pay your bills and shit?" Kaleem asked.

"Damn, playa, you all up in my shit, joker!" J-Money barked.

"Don't get defensive," injected Malik, "we're all just talking!"

"That's your little man?" Kaleem asked.

"Ya, that's my heart right there!"

"I feel ya, homie, I just know− our people, we should be tired of the misdeeds, incompetence, oppression, greed, corruption, and senseless killings."

"How about the guys down Camden Spanish Bryan and them doing their thing with the kids down there with North Camden Little League; they got the minor league Yankees, T-Ballers, Piraters, and Las Muñeca. They play at Poynt Park and Dominick Andujar Park."

"Let's ride down tomorrow and check them out," Mookie said to Dave.

"That's a bet."

Once Kaleem's cut was finished, they jumped in Hak's truck and left for the Honeycomb Hideout, an apartment in Orange. Absolutely none of the crew were allowed to bring anybody to the crib. This is where you could chill and collect your thoughts. Parking in the rear was a must.

***

The men made it to the spot. Hakim hooked the spot up with a touch of class fit for a king. Na'eem walked to the bar near the kitchen, pulling out three champagne glasses from the rack. He grabbed the fifth of Jonnie Walker 'Black Label'. Na'eem knew Kaleem would enjoy the smooth taste.

"Let's talk business," said Kaleem. "The cops gonna be trying to get at me."

"Yo, it ain't the same out here in the streets. They going by a different code don't seem to be a bond anymore."

"Speaking of the streets, a joker name Electro had four apartment buildings called The Paradice. He is eating heavy." said Hak.

"Ok, and?" asked Kaleem.

"People have been dying left and right. He has been using rat poison to cut his dope! He is a monster! You remember Sherri?"

Kaleem nods his head in agreement."She used to babysit me sometimes."

"Well, you wouldn't know her now," Hak told him.

"Hey, Hak, why you always moving the remote to the T.V?" Na'eem asked.

"I got it hooked up for voice command now. Check it out!" he began to use the voice command. "T.V on!" Click… it came on. "Show movie list, play movie 'Newark's Team'."

"Damn!" said Na'eem and Kaleem, spontaneously.

Na'eem poured the liquor and then made the toast, "Brick City, baby! Welcome home!" They let the smooth taste creep down their throats.

"I want to holla at ole boy Electro. I can see getting money, but rat poison!" stated Kaleem.

"You know, that could bring us to war with them," Na'eem replied.

"What you saying, we can't handle a war? Ain't no firepower anymore?"

"Firepower, bruh, the only things we don't have is tanks and planes!" boasted Hak.

Both men wanted to enlighten Kaleem. They treated each other like brothers. Kaleem fell into a daze thinking about how he would make his moves in the streets. One thing that made him happy other than Queen, was the fact that the charter school is touching the kids' lives!

Kaleem walked in the other room to make a few calls. *"I got to walk away from her."* he thought. Once again the pressure was on. He knew his life could be turned upside down at any given moment. He had to make moves and shake something. He dialed Queens number.

"Hello," Queen answered.

"Hello, beautiful. Queen, I've been thinking about my prior lifestyle and I know that it would be in your best interest that we no longer see each other. This is for your safety. So don't think it has anything to do with your health. You saw all the negative stuff they had on the news and in the papers."

"Really, Kaleem! So, last time I checked, I was a grown woman! I don't need you or anyone else to approve anything for me, sir!"

"I'm just saying."

"Mr. You got me twisted. You think you can turn me on and off anytime you like?"

"Honey, this isn't no fairy tale, people get killed, kidnapped, and even rapped. I don't want you to get hurt!" He felt the deed of rejection run through her veins.

"Not one day in the life is promised to anyone, and death will never be denied. I got to go. I'll call you later!"

"That's fine." he replied.

The next call he made was to Laton, the supervisor over ground maintenance at Newark Liberty International Airport. "Yo, star. Laton, this is Kaleem."

"What's going on?"

"I need your help setting up a party for me on the grounds at the airport."

"How big?"

"Big as two football fields; lights, action, six bars, and six swimming pools. Some of my people are making it happen."

"That's a lot. How soon you need it? I'ma have to get clearance for that!"

Listen, so that's no dilemma. I'ma drop you off ten stacks, so grease whatever palms need to be!"

"I'm on it!"

"Everyone attending will be instant messaged the event info."

Next, he texted, Mike of Extremely Dangerous Motorcycle Club: *Yo, Mike, hit me up.* He knew he could count on Mike's crew to help with security.

Kaleem opened up a text from Patrick: *Yo, kid, I got Illuztriouz Entertainment on the job promoting the party, James and Ty go hard.*

Everyone who was attending had to enter their email addresses. James and Ty set up a club fest website for location and rules. There were absolutely no pictures taken at the event. Straight, gays, lesbians, dots, anyone could attend.

Strachie got the word out about the party. People were excited to go, sending in thousand dollar deposits to reserve their spot. He strolls his email at the list of names...

1. Fire Links
2. Buju Banton
3. Busy Signal
4. Ishawana
5. Kaci
6. Boom Diva Dancers
7. Straight Edge
8. Big Beautiful Dancers
9. Big Girls Rock Dancers
10. Talent Flava
11. Moň Cherie... and more!

Newark's web page already had... Queen Latifah, Shack, Wyclef, Joe, Method Man, Redman, J-Lo, Naughty by Nature... and more!

Shaneeta from #1 Stunnas Instagram, her uncle, Kariem knew who was hosting the event. She called Kaleem and sure enough, the Jersey City Motorcycle Club #1 Stunnas would be attending as well. This event is sure to be nice and people are bound to come out in big numbers...

Chapter 8

Kaleem knew his next stop would be, Ms. Inez's place. She moved to Irvington to get away from the negativity that surrounded the death of Robo Cop. This little lady stayed busy. Kaleem wanted to have a private conversation with her concerning that night. Inez took extreme measures not knowing if he would kill both of them. Kaleem knew if it wasn't for her he would have been killed. The fear and danger lead this woman to take a life to save a life. Put in the same position, what would you do? *Hmm...*

"Let me put you on point, the cops got this thing called a 'stingray'," Hakim stated.

"Stingray," Kaleem repeated.

"Yeah, it's a briefcase size tracking system that picks up a person using their cell phone within feet. What it does is pose as a cell tower. This shit is illegal, so just keep a few phones with you."

"Ok, good looking. I'ma loose a lot of cell phones, I see."

"Yo, let's ride over to AK Ram's Cigar joint and Chill for a few." says Hakim.

"Man, I ain't seen him since the projects." said Kaleem.

"Yeah, he has a men's shelter also," Hak added.

"That's a blessing, giving back. Do they still have the concerts in Washington Park?"

"And you know that."

"Na'eem, how is your daughter Free doing?"

"Kaleem, I'm so proud of her. She is in her sixth year of college, about to be a lawyer."

"Damn, that's what's up! Now, all them haters can see you took care of her always and you're one of the best dads in the world."

"Thanks, man, she is my heart."

"Hey, Kaleem, he better have been a good dad, I'm the one trained him." Hakim joked, and everyone laughed.

"Kaleem, what happened to the girl from Newark named, Shawn, that you dated with the pretty dimples?"

"Wow, she was a good girl, I moved and we lost contact." Kaleem was feeling good from the drink. He hopped in the shower to freshen up. Na'eem hooked him up with a pair of Pelle jeans, forest green Timberlands, and a white-t. *"She could have been mine still."* he thought about her and how she treated him.

"We're going downtown to Source of Knowledge to check out the Black Men Do Read program they're having. We show our support to the only black-owned bookstore in Newark."

"That's what's up. Patrice still there?" asked Kaleem.

"Yeah, she's there," Na'eem replied.

Kaleem got dropped off at Ms. Inez's place…

***

Hearing the first-floor bell, after a brief minute, a soft-spoken voice says, "Who is it?"

"Kaleem!"

After looking out her side window, Inez opened the front door, holding her arms out for a hug. "Hi, baby," She didn't age much over the course of time. This woman carried the glow of sunshine anywhere she went.

"God Bless,"

"Whatever God Does is For the Best!"

"So right, so right," Kaleem replied.

"Come on in, I knew you were coming. You know I ain't cooked today."

"That's ok, I just wanted to talk to you alone. I'm not hungry."

"Have a seat."

"Thanks."

"Have you told your daughter what happened?"

"No, son, I have not and will not tell a soul. Only me and God knows! I have prayed and asked God to forgive me for all my sins. I did not intend for that cop to come into my home and do what he did to us that night."

"So what did you do with the gun?"

Ms. Inez walked over to the clock and opened it. Everything was there, the gun and the money.

"The money is yours, but I need to get rid of this, though." Referring to the gun. "Why did you say that at trial?"

"Why, because God has plans for you, and our bond will never be broken!"

46

"Of course not." he agreed. Snitching is never an option. People don't realize how the police play them, use them, and then put their lives and their families live's on the line because they can't do the job by themselves. Too many jokers put a dollar amount on their lives. You work for them, you get killed. They don't take care of your family, and they damn sure don't leave any pension or 401K for them.

"Kaleem, I just want you to take care of yourself."

"I want to keep your daughter safe too."

"Well, I know my daughter, and she ain't no little girl. Still, I don't want you to tell her what happened."

"I'ma tell you the truth, If I had not seen it with my own eyes, I wouldn't have believed it myself."

"The way he was hitting us in the face with his gun, he would have killed both of us, without a doubt!" she stated with confidence.

"I agree with you. Here, keep my number. My friends are outside to pick me up. If you need anything, just call me, I love you."

"Be safe, I love you, and know…" both of them spoke, "… Whatever God Does is For the Best!" they hugged before he left.

***

Kaleem jumped in the car with his boys, Na'eem and Hakim. They went by Marolo's, it was a Tuesday night and Vickey and her girls were magnets on getting people to come out and party. After some drinks and flirting, the men rode down to Club Atmosphere, still celebrating Kaleem's coming home. Kaleem had Queen on his mind. He knew he would always have a shadow following him. He wanted a better life than the one he had created.

Hakim introduced Na'eem and Kaleem to some kid named, Blaame. Blaame has a baby face hidden behind a full beard. A solid two hundred pounds and stood at five eight in height.

"What it do bruh?" asked Blaame. "Your Kaleem, right?"

"Yeah, what's the business?"

"Welcome home, bruh, that's what's up. Yo, if you need a trooper on your team get at your boy!"

47

"Blaame, no disrespect but, you're kind of young to be putting yourself out there like that." Kaleem preached. "I'm about to hit you with some real shit."

"Go ahead old school."

"Blaame, don't call me that and don't call me, nigga. That's cool with you?"

"My bad, no disrespect. Go ahead."

Trying to talk over the music, Kaleem moved in closer to Blaames ear. "How your mom and pops feel about you in the streets?"

"I take care of my own self. My father never stayed around, and then he got killed. I hated the fact that he never did things with me like, help me with my homework, sports, teach me about girls, show me how to protect myself, teach me how to drive, or even how to be a man. But the man part, I can't blame him much, because he didn't know either. I never heard, 'I'm proud of you, son.' Or 'I love you, son.' I will never get to ask him, was it me, something I did to make a father leave his kid. But, I got to love him, deadbeat and all!"

"Wow," Kaleem sat speechless for a second and then spoke. "Some things in life we may never get the answers to. One thing will help you…"

"What's that?" Blaame asked.

"Stay prayed up!"

"Yeah, ok, you too!" he responded with a smirk on his face.

After Blaame walked off, Kaleem asked Hak, "What's up with that dude? It was something about the kid that gave me chills, but what in the world is it?"

"I met him in the county and liked the joker. Some guys thought they could take his canteen, but got a rude awakening. He had a can lid that opened up both of the guys face like he was a doctor."

"Damn, yeah!"

"Yeah, they violated the rule… No stealing, and to keep the heat from out the dorm."

"Like I said, it's something, I just can't put my finger on it!"

Chapter 9

Kaleem put insurance back on his Honda Accord, which was still in great shape and looking good. He picked Queen up to take her to dinner in New York City's Village. As he pulled up, she was already waiting outside of her place, glowing with joy. "Hi, Kaleem."

"Hello, beautiful." He leaned over to kiss her glossy lips as she got in. "Where are we going again? That kiss wiped my memory out."

"Boy, cut it out... To get something to eat."

"Ok, I'm good now." He pushed play on the car stereo and Howard Hewett was playing, For the Lover in You. "Do you remember this song, Queen?"

"Well of course. How could I forget our trip to Atlantic City?" She reached over, held his right hand, and placed it on her thigh. He squeezed her thigh, sending chills up and down her body. She became moist, feeling the heat from her kitten. "Kaleem, this seems so unreal, seeing you again. Many nights I have prayed this day would come. I always wanted to know, why wouldn't you let me visit you?"

"I didn't want to take either of us through that. I didn't want you to feel pressured like you owed me anything. Plus, you could have had a change of heart."

"The only change in my heart was that I wanted you more! Speaking of the court system, I felt like they took away a part of me when they took you. I did not date nor have I slept with a man still!"

"How about a woman?"

"Kaleem, I am serious!"

"I'm just joking, my bad."

"I'm not Kaleem, let me finish. I have so much going on right now. Some guys gave money to build a top of the line school for kids in the Central Ward District."

"That was a beautiful thing. What's the name of it?"

"The Charter School for Kings and Queens. As a matter of fact your lawyer, Mr. DeValle is a key player with it. You know I have been training with the KA system, I enjoy Kevin's karate classes."

"Are you any good?"

"Let's say, I'm a GI-Jane." they both laughed.

"Queen, my hand is getting hot on your thigh."

"My oven gets hot like that." She placed his hand right on her hot box.

"Damn!" his manhood began to rise, steering his car back into his lane after a car blew their horn, warning Kaleem that he was about to cause an accident.

***

The setting, authentic with a menu showcasing food flavor of Spanish Culture. Queen and Kaleem agreed on the Paella Valencia, a great seafood, and yellow rice meal. The waiter brought Queen a large Piña Colada and Kaleem a Captain Morgan Spiced Rum and Sprite. The soft homemade bread was warm enough to melt the butter that they'd spread over it.

"Kaleem, I can only imagine what my moms and you went through that night. That experience changed all of our lives." She began to cry. "I'm sorry, excuse me." She got up and went to the restroom.

He sat there admiring her shapely figure. She was wearing a sheer stripe jumpsuit with a V-neck cut. Her booty jiggled as she stepped In her Kenneth Cole heels.

She returned to the table just as the food was arriving. "So, Mr., how does it feel to be free?"

"Well, from behind bars and gates, great! But as long as the judicial system stays the way it is, no people of color will be free. Until they make the people of the court accountable for their misconduct on, producing false evidence, lying, and doing whatever it takes just to convict someone, and when they are exposed, they face no consequences, because under the Supreme Court created a doctrine called 'absolute immunity' so nothing happens to them. And guess what? How in the hell is that fair?"

"I agree with you on that! Now, what about us, Kaleem? That's what I want to talk about. I know while going after your dreams in life you go through the roughness, the struggle, the obstacles, and some never stop looking at the big picture. You have a purpose and through your labor, you can make the difference in someone's life. It's essential that you follow me, let there be no dilemma in your mind. I have a purpose for being with you. I don't know how much longer GOD's gonna have me on this earth, still, I choose to live life to the fullest. I am grateful every single day. When I look into your eyes, I see my soul companion, when I hear your voice, it cuts into me like a razor of joy. I know it's part of you that will never lose its mystery… And that just makes me want you more. So don't discriminate on me, I'm a big girl, now, and am ready for whatever life has for me."

"I don't want you to eat those words. Queen, I don't know when someone may kill me or I may have to kill someone. I don't want you to get killed!"

She leaned in closer to him and said, "Let me die knowing I was with the man I gave my life too." Kaleem's eyes filled with tears, he got himself together as she gave him a kiss. She continued, "My trust, you gained that, my love, you earned that, my heart, you own that, your bust it chick, I'll be that, and if I have to kill, I'll do that, just to be with you, yes baby, even that!"

"Wow, Queen, what are you doing to me? You blew my mind with what you just said. I'm not gonna front, I played the streets, I sold drugs, used drugs, and mentally hurt women. I have awakened to the fact that I did not understand me! Learning to be a man is a daily experience. You can't be a man and make boy decisions. Your choices and actions will reflect who you are. Will I fall short at times? Yes! Will I protect you? Yes! Will I love you? Yes!"

"That's all I'm asking, Kaleem. I see the party has got social media jumping."

"It's ILLIZTRIOUZ ENTERTAINMENT, James, and Ty, they do release parties, promo parties, bookings, and book signings for new release artist. They go hard in the paint."

"What is go hard in the paint?"

"They really work hard at what they do. So, I hope you're coming!"

"I want to, but my supervisor at work is a devil. I know she wakes up thinking how to make my life miserable. If I can get off, I will attend."

The two finished eating, left and drove to see the One World Trade Center.

***

Kaleem knew their presence here at the One World Trade Center would be touching in terms of emotion. Standing at 1,776 feet the breathtaking building stood in illumination. The led modules seem to light up the sky!

"Isn't it beautiful?" asked Kaleem.

"Yes, it is, honey. Can we take a moment to reflect on the many families' lives that have been affected by 911?"

"That's a great idea, Queen." They both closed their eyes and neither said a word for a few minutes.

"Thank you, Kaleem." They both opened their eyes.

Queen had to be at work at 6 a.m. Kaleem was a complete gentleman and gave her a hug and kiss, and then left to get some rest himself.

Chapter 10

It's one week before the ceremony at the charter school. A meeting was about to take place, but it wasn't about the school. Donesha is the principal and all the kids loved her. She carried a spirit of love everywhere she went. The ladies mostly from Scudder Home projects got together to form a plan because of many senseless killings that had caused so many Newark residents to be buried. They came to terms that they needed to be a part of the solution.

Shavonne taught all of the girl's hand to hand combat techniques over the last two summers. She traveled around the world for ten years teaching women how to protect themselves. She was in top shape and could get along with anyone around. Pamela, Ayesha, Sonya, and Mika were down. They knew Dena and Shonda wouldn't be left out. Zikirrah is the gym teacher, a chocolate petite size model chick with an attitude. If you cross her the wrong way, look out! Latrise ran the Brain Power Leadership program. She always wanted to give back, so she moved from Jersey City to be a part of the school. Long hair, hazel eyes, classy, and had no problem fitting right in. So don't let the looks fool ya! Then there is Khayyirrah, a light skin, curvy, solid, pretty face diva. Her dressing game was so fierce the students called her, Ms. Hollywood. They all took their jobs seriously and could go from zero to sixty in no time! Their goal was to make things better for the students even if they had to take things into their own hands.

Pat brought Queen and Niecy with her. Niecy played no games if you crossed her also. Most of the girls were raised together and made a bond that no matter what happens or what religion anyone became, they would never forget the community.

Donesha stood up and raised her hand to get everyone's attention. "Good evening, everyone!"

"Hi, D." the girls sang in unison.

"I want you all to know that you were highly recommended and picked for this job because of who you are and what you are about. At the end of this meeting, if you choose not to partake in this matter, you will keep what went down here tonight to yourselves! Or you will feel the wrath! We will be pro-active, we will be organized, we will set priorities, and we will eliminate clutter! We are tired of our young men killing each other. Many of them are lost and confused. Many feel they are trapped into destroying their lives, because of an oath they took. This is how much they are willing to be loved, to take care of the life of another. To take away someone's loved one. We are going to make a statement that we've had enough! Please, hear Shavonne out…"

"Hi, ladies, this is the game plan… We know there are only two gangs that run the city, the Young Mafia Crew and the Avenues. We are going to cripple them by stealing their weapons!" Shavonne stated.

"What!" Ayesha screamed.

"That's right, take their weapons. You got to understand that both groups have a large arsenal of weapons. I'm talking, 50" calibers, AK-47's, 223 rifles, and handguns."

"How are we going to do that, just walk right in and ask them?" Sonya stated sarcastically.

"Not exactly…" Shavonne went on, "Dena, you need to get in touch with, Lena."

"Why?"

"Because Lena owns three apartment buildings and the house on Keer Ave, is one of the stash houses for guns."

"What about the other?" Pat asked.

"That's on Twelfth Ave. You see only one guy monitors that, so guess how we're getting inside?" Donesha stated.

"Pay him?" Mika asked.

"Kidnap him?" asked Dena.

"Sort of, kind of, it's the power of the coochie! The majority of men think with the head between their legs, which makes them suckers. One way to get your man's attention is to stop having sex with him! Only two things can happen, he will either work it out with you or go find a side chick. So, with that being said, I need all of you to abstain from sex for the next two weeks." Donesha told the ladies.

"Damn!" said Pamela. "Does eating count?" the women all laughed.

"Yeah, it counts. I want everyone's thinking to be at its best and with all your strength." Shavonne said strongly.

"We need for our *Black Kings* to start back protecting the *Black Queen* and not destroy them. We need to build them up and not put them down..." said Zikirrah as she went on, "I'm looking forward to Kaleem's party. All of Scudder Home girl's going to represent! Hotels are filling to the max, from New Brunswick to New York, my ass going to stay dancing!" boasted Zikirrah.

"Yeah, you can dance, girl," Shonda added.

Both Sonya's attended the meeting, one from Lincoln and the other from Howard. Both ladies are beautiful, intelligent, and sexy. Sonya from Howard carried a baby 380 Ruger gun; she shot her boyfriend in the chest for slapping her; So, we call her, Little 380, so she will use it!

"When does all this jump off?" Dena inquired.

"The same night Kaleem's party is jumping off," Donesha said.

"Now, Queen, that's where you come in. We want you to let us know where it's going to be soon as you find out. Everybody will be waiting to be hit up on every social media platform. Everyone will be V.I.P that night. So we want to make sure we are seen there." said Pat.

"I can handle that," Queen replied.

Donesha began speaking. "Y'all know Mike the Dike Dixon wants all the Scudder Home women to roll inside with him at the party. He will pay for twenty-five outfits from head to toe. So let me know and it's done."

"Now, is there anyone of you that doesn't feel they can handle this?" asked Donesha. She scanned the room to find none of the women's hands raised. "I'll take that to say, we all will go the extra mile to make this work. I have in front of you the information on what everyone is to do. We have three hours left in this meeting. Memorize your position so I can get rid of all the paperwork!"

"Girl, I hope that two weeks of no sex don't start tonight, 'cause I'ma try to break my beau's back tonight!" boasted Khay.

"That's what I'm saying." Pam agreed.

"Ladies, I feel what y'all saying, but on the real, make sure you take this job seriously. I want all of us to walk out those two houses the same way we went in. And I pray we don't have to kill none of them!" Shavonne said.

"How are we supposed to stop the killing if we end up killing someone?" asked Ayesha.

Donesha injected, "That will be a sacrifice we must endure to make the future better for our community!"

"I'm not gonna be playing with anyone, I'm coming home to my boys!" Dena said.

"I want to go with y'all too," Queen stated.

"Hell no! We need your eyes and ears at the party to verify everything is good. As long as our timing is together, we are good." said Pat.

"Y'all know one of the young girls that worked for Pretty Ricky back in the day before he got killed... Well, the girl name is, Lisa, and she is graduating from college this year." Lashonda said.

"Now, that's what's up!" Pam stated.

"That shows you how anybody can change their lives for better," Ayesha said.

"Ok, girls don't mention this to no one. Are we going to do this?" Donesha asked.

In unison, all the ladies agreed and said, "Yes!"

"Ok..." Pam began to speak, "this concludes our meeting. Go get your backs broke or break his, and then after that shut it down, and remember, it's power in the coochie!"

The ladies burst out in laughter!

Chapter 11

It's seven o'clock and the weather is beautiful outside. The kids and parents filled the auditorium at the banquet for the Kings and Queens Charter School.

"If everyone can take a seat, we could get started, thank you! Hello, my name is, Ms. Walker, and I'm, proud to say, I'm one of the directors in this program. We have two more directors, which are also good friends of mine... Momma Dixon and Marie Ward, please, show some love." The crowd clapped. "Now, I would like you to meet our principal, Donesha!"

"Hi, my people, tonight we will speak on quite a few subjects. So, I ask that you give your undivided attention and listen attentively, please. First up is Darren, he will read one poem to you. Please welcome him!"

"Hello, my pen name is, D. WritersBlock...
Poetry is something you can relate to
Poetry is something you can snap your fingers to
Poetry is something you feel inside
Poetry is passion, paint pictures with her words
Poetry is like music, gets a good vibe from her words
Poetry hits the soul
Poetry is smooth and romantic, feel her flow
Poetry is my friend, that's why I'm close to her
Poetry is love, that's why I married her
Poetry makes me think, Poetry gives me chills
When I wanna escape, I turn to my poetry."
The crowd applauded, loving what they heard!
"Next up is, Ja'Dare, pen name HOP."
"Thank you, this is the pass I want you to catch...

Go deep into the manufacturing company that manufactures the pen that supplied the ink, that allowed me to apply the words on the paper that my mind supplied.

Go deep into the earth that supplied the trees that the paper needed to accomplish this piece.

Go deep into the essence of my equality and possibility.

Go deep into my heart and find the importance of my love.

Go deep into my words and find the urge of silence. The concern of my words creates a timeless zone. As I go deep into the relevance in some of my actions.

Go deep and see what barely scratch the surface.

Go deep and see my bravery, go deep I can see death always await.

Go deep into tomorrow and uncover the hidden lives of yesterday.

Go deep into the centuries preserved so well, listen to the many stories they know so well, Martin, Assata, Tubman, Huey, Parks, Malcolm, and Angelou, what courage they carried. I can have that same courage, can't I?

Go deep into the youth with proof of leadership and a positive message. Make lessons of knowledge.

Go deep into meditation without hesitation.

Go deep, can you catch?"

The crowd was hit hard by Ja'Dare with his powerful words of wisdom.

"Thank you," he said to the crowd before walking off the stage.

Next, Khayyirrah took the mic. "I'm Khay, for short. Even though the kids call me, Ms. Hollywood as she smiled knowing why. I have a poem by my niece, Tynila."

"America the Land of the Free,
How can this be?
They can't be speaking of me,
Remember when you set your laws in place,
You didn't count me because of the color of my face.
You stole attempting to break our souls,
How could something be found that was never lost,
The truth must be told!
You say equal rights, so why must we still fight?
If you handcuff yourself to hatred, you become a hater, and you become angry.
All I want to do is live the same way you want to…
Thank you!"

"Wow, that was awesome!"

Kaleem came in and found his seat next to Mamma Hutch. She greeted him with a smile and a hug. He spotted Queen on the stage, sitting in her True Religion jean suit. Kaleem was dressed down in Timbs and jeans.

Pam stepped on the podium and got the microphone. "Good evening! We must want to grow, decide to grow, and make an effort to grow. It is a blessing for us to have this school. We will see the girls and guys grow into productive men and women seeking higher education. Yes, we as a group of people have been through some tragic events concerning, police, not only does Black Lives Matter but All Lives Matter! We must overcome by pulling in the same direction. This way we can make a difference. Thank you for your time." The crowd clapped.

Queen came to the stage and gave Pam a hug and began to speak. "Hello, beautiful people! I'm Queen, and tonight I would like to share a few things with you all. Sometimes we have to go through things in life, we stumble and fall, and pick ourselves back up, and ask ourselves, what just happened and why? Before we could really start to understand things and somewhere in all that turmoil, we began to see that we have a purpose in this lifetime. I want to speak to you about AIDS because I am positive!" the crowd was in shock. She continued. "You can't place a face on this virus. My focus is to give information and support. It has been 30 years since AIDS first began killing people. It is evident we must not give up the fight. The treatment of AIDS in the last decade has been a major success. Let's take the time to thank the many men, women, and kids who gave their lives trying to find a cure. To the countless doctors and scientist fighting to produce a vaccine for the virus, that is diabolical as well as evolving. Black women account for 70% of the new HIV cases among women. The importance of getting tested and knowing your status is a must! Know your partner! Please take advantage of the many websites, creating conversations online concerning this epidemic. Women, as well as men, should value their bodies. So I urge you tonight to further your education, you are our future. One last thing I want you to remember as humans, we have been blessed with super intelligence, we can accumulate, remember, and evaluate masses of information. We possess qualities not only of consciousness but self-awareness as well. We long for significance and goals. Always keep pushing and you will get results! Thank you!" Everyone stood to their feet and clapped.

"Simply elegant," Kaleem said as he walked up to Queen and hugged her. "I don't get a kiss?"

"Kaleem!"

"Kaleem, what?"

"Here," She kissed his lips.

"Why thanks." he said with a smile.

"Listen, it's girls night out, so call me tomorrow, please, if you can."

"Ok, be careful and keep it tight, alright."

"Keep what tight?" she asked, confused.

"You know!"

"Yeah, ok, don't play with me like that. Call me sweetie, good night!"

"Good night."

Queen kept her plans with her girls. They enjoyed the turnout tonight. Kaleem called it an early night and went to the Honeycomb Hideout to chill.

Chapter 12

Kaleem drove to the airport to pick up his old partner, Ta'Rod. There was no way he would stay in Kansas when he found out his dude had come home. Kaleem knew that doing time you got to realize it's a cold world and the word love is not always an action word.

Kaleem saw Ta'Rod walking out of terminal 'C' of the airport. "Yo, yo!" they embraced each other with a strong manly hug.

"Man, you still have that damn Honda? It still looks good, I got to give you that."

"I haven't driven it in four years, plus, it only has fifteen thousand miles on it."

"Damn, I'm glad your home man. You know Kansas City is jumping. Whites and Blacks get along down there."

"That's the way it should be all over, but it's a lot of people that inherit stupidity and refuse to innovate. You hungry, Ta'Rod?"

"Sure, it doesn't matter where we go."

"Cool. Down on Clay St, Jay-Z moms have a spot called Diamondz N Da Ruff Café and Lounge. It's straight."

"That's a bet. So, bruh, all social media is talking about ya party. I see people from all over coming."

"Yeah, a couple of my dudes putting in work to make it jump off."

They arrived at the restaurant… A nice family atmosphere. They took a table and both ordered, steak dinners and drinks.

"Man, I told you, we should have got rid of Robo Cop." Ta'Rod implied.

"Yeah, I can see that, now. That cocaine had his brain gone. God wasn't' ready for me yet! I saw my life pass right in front of me. So, I came to grips that God's got a plan for me and it's not what I've been doing."

"Kaleem, whatever happened to that nurse? She had you gone!"

"Yeah, right. For your information, she is around."

"Well, did you get the goodies?"

"What does it matter, you ain't get any!" Kaleem shot back.

"Trust me, I don't want none of that package," Ta'Rod added.

"Yo, we gonna leave Queen out of our conversations from now on!"

"Easy, bruh, no problem."

"So, you still in the business?" asked Kaleem.

"You know I am, but not like we were. Why, you ready to turn up?"

"Hell no! I got to help people. I gave mostly all my cash to build a school."

"What!"

"Yeah, they just had a program last week. It's doing really well too."

"That's what's up. Excuse me, waitress!" Ta'Rod called.

"Yes, how can I help you?"

"Two more drinks and our bill, please."

"Sure, I'll be right back."

"Hold up, is that Salideen from Broome St.?" Kaleem walked over to the solidly built bodybuilding guy. "Excuse me, is your name Sal?"

"Yeah, why?"

"Homie, our family lived on Broome together; the Wards, Long's, and Dixons."

"Word. As-Salaam-Alaikum. I know all of them. I love me some Maxine and Wanda.

"Wa-Laikum-Salaam. You used to watch me play football in the Hank Aaron field."

"Yeah, you were a little dude back then, but you loved running that ball and hitting."

"How you been?" Kaleem asked.

"I got messed up down South Carolina."

"Word, they still racist down there!"

"You're right about that. They'll do anything to get a conviction, no matter what! You know they were the last to abolish slavery? With 32 prisons, they have the balls and the audacity to question the overcrowding. They don't let people go and lock you up for jaywalking."

"Yo, this my man, Ta'Rod."

"As-Salaam-Alaikum, I'm Sal."

"Wa-Laikum-Salaam."

"Here you go." The waitress passed the check to Ta'Rod.
He handed her a hundred dollar bill. "Keep the change."
"Thank you!" she replied.
"No, thank you!"
"Check this out, Sal here is my info. Next week my peeps are having me a welcome home party. Come check me out!"
"That's a bet."
"You ready, Ta'Rod?" Kaleem asked.
"Ok, As-Salaam-Alaikum," Sal told them.
"Wa-Laikum-Salaam." Ta'Rod and Kaleem both replied.

As Kaleem and Ta'Rod walked down the block to the car, Kaleem noticed a black BMW with smoked out tinted windows coming to a slow creep. They see the driver's window coming down fast, but it seems to be in slow motion until the sounds of a large caliber gun ejected bullets, shattering glass and going through metal. The men ran for their lives to duck for cover. The driver sped off not wanting to get caught but didn't hit his targets.
"Damn, you alright?" Kaleem mumbled.
"Who in the hell was that?"
"How the hell I know? Let's roll before the police come asking questions." Kaleem said.
Both of their heart rates were running fast and sweating as if a bucket of water was thrown on them.
"Man, drop me off on Orange Ave, at my man Kaleef's house so I can get me a gun and a vehicle while I'm here."
"Ok. That Beemer got to be stolen, so ain't no use in looking for that." Kaleem drove Ta'Rod to his boy's spot and dropped him off. "Aye, Ta'Rod, I'ma drive down Princeton and chill for a few days."
"Ok, just get at me."
After cutting his phone off and removing the battery, Kaleem went to the Hyatt Regency Hotel. He ordered drinks and kicked back to get his thoughts together.

Chapter 13

"Hey, Lena."

"Hi, Dena, what's up, girl?"

"Well, you know your house on Keer Avenue?"

"Yeah, what about it?"

"Well, the first-floor apartment is where the Avenue gang keeps their guns!"

"What!"

"Yes, girl, so I need that front door key and diagram of the apartment."

"Dena, them guys are crazy! I don't want to have my name involved with them."

"Listen, you ain't got to be worried 'bout that!" Dena told her.

"Girl, promise me... I mean, put your bond on it." she said as she was taking the key off the ring.

"Word is bond, Lena! Stop tripping, you never knew me to tell anything."

"Here is the key and the diagram of how the rooms are in the house. I don't know anything!"

"Good, keep it that way. I got it from here, thanks, girl."

"Be careful," Lena said as they embraced each other with a hug.

Dena left to meet up with the other girls.

***

Dena met Ayesha at her house. Sonya's friend worked for the gas and electric company PSE&G, so Sonya was able to get some uniforms and use his truck.

"Pam is going to meet us near Keer Ave," Ayesha stated.

Khay has been staking out the apartment for the last four hours, so far only two guys are in the apartment.

"You get the key for the front door?" Ayesha asked.

"C'mon, I got that covered, girl," Dena replied.

"Ok, everybody ready?" Sonya asked as she and Dena put on their uniforms.

Sonya pulls the utility truck right in front of the apartment. The girls jumped into action; Dena put the cones out on the street to slow down traffic, plus they didn't want to be blocked in. Donesha got the front door from Dena and went into the apartment building and sprayed a solvent that gave off an odor of gas fumes, and then walked back outside. The girls checked their two-way radios to make sure that they worked and were charged. Immediately Sonya and Dena went into action and rang the doorbell...

Ring... Ring... Ring...

Someone peeked out the blinds, the first thing they noticed was the lights flashing from the truck. "Who is it?" was a strong, demanding voice behind the door.

"PSE&G, we're here to check a gas line leak."

"Hold on− Yo Buttons, close that bedroom door, the gas people here to check a leak." said Rob.

"Ok, let them in so they can hurry and go, I'm ready to smoke a loud blunt." said Buttons.

"Hello," Rob spoke as he let Dena and Sonya in the front door. He walked them into the apartment. "I smell the gas now! Damn, they got some sexy women working for them now."

"Equal rights for women in effect. How long has this odor been here?" asked Sonya.

"Yo, Button, check out who they sent out to check our gas leak!"

This was surely a stash house hangout spot. Clothes all over the place, sneakers and boots all on the floor, an Xbox and a big screen TV.

"Ladies, ladies." said Buttons after looking them up and down.

"Hi," both ladies spoke.

"Can someone show me the kitchen, please?" asked Sonya.

"Sure, I got you." Buttons lead the way.

Rob grabbed Dena's hand and told her to wait with him. "Don't ever touch me again!" she said while pulling her hand away.

"Damn, you a little firecracker, huh? Easy, I just wanna holla at you for a few. Do you smoke?"

"Yeah," Dena said, lying.

"Hold on…" Rob went in the room to get a blunt. When he walked back into the living room, Dena had her back turned and when she turned around, she had her gun pointed at Rob.

"Quietly," she said. "Nice and slow get on your knees," she told him. "Did you find the leak!" she yelled to Sonya. That told Sonya to get control.

Sonya pulled her gun out her tool bag and walked Buttons back in the living room. "We clear." she spoke in the two ways, letting Ayesha and Pam know that they had things under control and for them to come inside. With duffle bags in hand, the girls went straight into the back room and began loading up the guns.

Rob is two hundred and thirty pounds and the baddest out the two men. "I hope y'all know we're members of the Avenue gang and somebody gonna pay for this shit!" he stated.

Slap! Dena's gun came crashing across Rob's face, allowing his front tooth to fall out as he spat blood from his mouth.

Pam and Ayesha were on their third trip cleaning out the room. Dena and Sonya tied the two guys hands and feet up.

Slap! Sonya came across Button's face. "What the hell you do that for?" he asked.

"Because when we leave you're gonna tell ya boy, 'I wish she would have hit me like that' so I stopped that!" she said nastily.

Both girls had a smirk on their face, forcing themselves to laugh. The girls got what they came for and rolled out. They changed clothes and put the truck back like it never left.

***

Over on Twelfth Avenue, the Junior Mafia Crew kept their guns at Tommy's place. The word got out that Tommy was a freak that loved a pretty face and a smile. Shavonne got her cousin from Washington D.C name, Kyiesha. She had no problem taking on the task. Solid built, 5'9" milk chocolate complexion, he played no games with over twenty-five knockouts, she was the go-to chick. Shavonne, Shonda, and Zookie filled Kyiesha in on her job and she was ready.

"Hey, Shavonne, you know I still want that Gucci bag I asked you for?" Keyshia questioned.

"Girl, somebody stole that damn bag. I see you are still on your diva game."

"I guess you can say that. Now, if this joker doesn't want to comply you know what's up." Kyiesha added. She will not be playing once she is inside.

"Ok, you know the game plan, right?" asked Zookie.

"Yeah, yeah, yeah, I got it!" Kyiesha replied.

"Good, I'll be waiting on you at the corner."

"I love you, cuz. Handle your business, girl." Shavonne told her.

"Relax, money in the bag," Kyiesha said as she got out the car. She walked down the street to Tommy's place. The building boasted a brown stucco front, music pumped from the cars riding by, and the horns blew as some drivers saw her. But she kept it moving, knowing she had a job to perform. When she approached the door, she rang the doorbell...

Tommy looked out the window from behind the shade. Seeing the curvy, chocolate female in his view, he automatically wanted to ring her bell. "What can I help you with, beautiful?"

"Hi, is K.K home?"

"She will be back in a few." Tommy lied just to keep up the conversation. "What's your name, honey?"

"I'm sorry, I'm Niki. What's yours?"

"Big Man," Tommy replied.

"Big Man," Kyiesha repeated.

"Why you say it like that, something wrong with my name?"

"No, my bad. It's that you don't look like no Big Man." she said with a sexy smile.

"Well, don't let the looks fool ya, baby girl. You want to come inside and have a drink until K.K gets back?"

"Got him!" Kyiesha thought to herself, knowing he was tricking her into the house. He didn't know it was just what she came to do. "I don't want to impose on you and your company, just tell her to call Niki."

"No, I don't have company and it's no bother, come on in."

They walked inside. He kept a clean place. A woman's touch with plants, pictures on the walls, and new furniture. The paint on the living room walls was beige with dark brown trim. 'Again' by

Fetty Wap played in the background, a kid from Jersey that was blowing up the airwaves.

Tommy had only one thing on his mind, and that was getting her clothes off. He put some liquid ecstasy inside her drink and waited for it to mix and dissolve while asking questions from the kitchen. "So, where you from, Niki?"

"East Orange." she lied.

Kyiesha wasn't a slow leak, she knew not to drink from anything she didn't see the seal broken off the bottle. She would never leave her drink unattended at a club after her girlfriend Taz was gang raped after a guy slipped a date rape drug called Ketamine in her drink.

Tommy thought that she would be an easy prey and retrieve her goodies without her consent. He attempted to pass her the champagne glass. He stood in his tracks as Kyiesha sprayed his face full of mace. He dropped both of the glasses and took a wild swing that landed directly into her jaw.

She yelled. "Damn!" he continued to throw wild punches hoping to connect again. She shook off the punch and kicked him between his legs crushing both of his testicles bringing him to his knees as he hollers, and then she kneed him in his face knocking him unconscious. A few more kicks to the face and more mace just because she was now in control. She knew to act fast with her eyes tearing from the mace. She called Shavonne, Mika, and Zook to come with the duffle bags.

The girls rushed into the apartment. Mika zipped tied and gagged Tommy making sure he wouldn't be a problem. None of the girls could handle the powerful effect of mace in the air. They quickly loaded up the guns and were gone in no time. They all met up and loaded all the stolen guns into a stolen Yukon Pam had popped up the night before. Queen drove as the girls followed with their guns. They drove the guns to Green St., by the police station and left. "Black Live Matter to us!" the ladies said, giving each other high fives.

Chapter 14

It's party time! All the sites have been jumping, Facebook, Twitter, IG, Snapchat, Instant Messenger, Skype, Tango, and What's Up... Of course, you had your last minute shoppers rushing to the malls to look their best. The airport grounds had been set up as Laton had directed. Six swimming pools; two that are foam pools, six bars, ten bathrooms, and metal detectors. The color theme is gold and white, set up by Alexis Mia Creations. The entrance into the area will begin at six p.m.

Shanita, Supe, Bug, and NewNew lead the pack of more than fifteen riders of the #1 Stunnas of the North Jersey Chapter out of Jersey City. They got on the Turnpike to meet with the Redline Motorcycle Club at entry 14 of the Turnpike. Riding with Redline was, Kareem (Hickey), Jazzy, Vince, Reese, and Johora turning the gas to meet up. Extremely Dangerous, MC Club followed suit with their president Mike, followed by Rah 1000, Dee Money, Bolo, and Stitch. All the motorcycle clubs rode down the Turnpike to meet up with the Lost Boys, Myrtle Beach Chapter at the beginning of the Turnpike. All the clubs rode as professionals and organized, using hand signals, front-leaders, back-men, blockers, and headsets.

AK-Ram of the famous 6one9 Cigar Lounge in Newark will be in charge of keeping the six bars filled with lots of liquor and cigars. The DJ's were all setting up with the speakers that were supplied by Pioneer. Four tractor-trailers were parked on the outskirts, resting on top of them are four one hundred inch projector screens, so patrons would see themselves partying tonight. Big Jodi called Supe to inform him that the Lost Boys would be rolling up at exit 1 of the Turnpike in about fifteen minutes.

Supe turned up the speed and all the other groups done the same. Just as the Lost Boys were in line to pay the toll, they could see the more than two hundred biker headlights roaring down the south side of the Turnpike. That was enough time for Buddy, Jodi, Bleeze, Slim, Fats, Tracey, Kendrick, Backwood, Shocka, Tim, Eligha, J-Black, and all the other riders to stretch their legs. All four motorcycle clubs were burning up the New Jersey Turnpike doing some hard riding; cutting in between cars and trucks, riding the shoulders and doing wheelies. Nash showed out by wheeling from Exit 1 to Exit 14 while changing lanes and using his signal lights; this man was made to ride. This was the way Jersey welcomed the Lost Boys. Making it to the airport in twenty-five minutes showed the bikes were flying. The bikes came thundering, chrome down, shining colors, and lights to the sound of pipes! The bikes went into motion surrounding the event as planned.

People began packing the party at all four entrances. Everyone attending will have their curiosity satisfied tonight. New Jersey, New York, Jamaica, VA, Philly, Conn, Cali, NC, SC, ATL, Florida, Canada, Panama and more. Patrick and Strachie made sure everything ran smooth. Red and Yolanda made sure no one had problems with their tickets. Boom Diva Dancers, Busy Signal, Chicken Chest, Dellie, Body Guard, Cutchie, Straight Edge Dancers, Kaci along with eighty more patrons from the Island. The Jamaican DJ's Pink Panther and Fire Links were ready to blaze the dance floor. DJ Na'eem Johnson, DJ Kasper, DJ Hunter, J Moo, and DJ Mona Lisa were all ready to move the crowd. New York spinning music on deck is Red Alert, Chuck Rock, and DJ BedRock. Newark was coming hard with, Redman, Treach, Queen Latifah, Busta Rhymes, Vinney, KG, Jahiem, Joe, Lauryn Hill, Shaq, Wyclef, Wendy W, Madonna, and Taylor S. Naughty by Nature was the first rap artist to take home a Grammy Award.

Scudder Homes Crew came out in big numbers to show love to one of their own. Kat, Jackie, Chicken, Tiny, Sha-freakqua, Lynn, Lulu, Diane, Coonie, Sonnie, Clara, Shelia C, Faye and Shelia, Vanessa, Rakeemah, Gloria, Ruby, Alfreda, Janice, Bernice, Yakeema, Grier, Tina, Alnesha (Poohie), Sharan (Suggs), Sissy-Gal, Constance, Ayesha, Mika, Felicia, Debra, Delfine, Sucriss, Penny, Haneefah, Pauline, Pam, Kim, Shaboom, Gloria, Lisa, Shorty, Porgy, Fishcake, China, Dianne, Jazz, Fatisha, Amerah, Amenah, Patsy, Lena, Dew, Valerie, Evette, Mary, Tonia, Towanna, Dionne, Linda, Jean, Sha, Narrow, Pamela, Tanisha, Alma, Regina, Wanda, Beeah, Hafee, Ronda, Elouise, Vanessa, Sandra, Virgina, Renee, Rose, Sybil, Fern, Queenie, Helen, Kha, Zook, Niecy, Stacey, Shaheeda, and so many others ladies.

Many more pouring in were, Rodolph, Gary, Pluck, Shawny, Marky, HotRod, Charles (Red), Barry, Shaheed, Omar 'Poochie',

Omar 'Smiley', Balil, Shariff, Big-Will, John, Al-Biseah, Clark, Terrance, Hannibal, Handbone, Gary, Chris, Greg, Salaam, Sapp, Jamel, Hafeez, Spoony, Quadir, Ant Man, Fuquan, Qenzell, D.C, Tye, Blood, Zookie, Ricky, CB, Moose, Hassie, Dexter, Bodeen, Short, AB, Johnny AB, Thomas, Glen, Wite White, Wali, Hakeem, Tariq, Theodore, Biseem, Jamal, K.B, Derek, KD, Fudent, Chase, Tiny-Tim, Bone, Twin, Nawty, Herbie, Keefie, Reggie, Brian, Sal, Masharod, Manny, Wayney, Melvin, Bud, Button, Rasheed, Ali, Lil Rick, Boda-boot, Terrence, Al Smooth, and many more... Just to mention!

The fever crew, East Crew of New York, George that made 'Game People Play' song! Keith and Kevin, Squeek, Nigil, Rich, Paul, Mustafah, Musiquah, Ray, Charles, Haywood, Fred, Handbone, Meatball, Pookie, Bernice, Johna, Mia Irving, Ralf, Jamila, Saleem, Bosey (Bass-Man), Ali Mu, June, Tempest, Bennitta, Ena, Ariana, Mia, Pat, Sandra, and much more!

People are still waiting in line as the party fills up...

The MC took the mic. "People, people, what's up! I'm your host MC tonight, I'm Michael aka Rippa MC, and I want to big ups to everyone that's out tonight. Let's shout and welcome home, Kaleem!" the crowd went into a frenzy with applause. "Guy, we better thank God for all these beautiful women we are seeing tonight. And ladies, you have some choices to make tonight, these guys are at their best!" The crowd began clapping. "Let's shout out, Illuztriouz Entertainment, Ty and James Illogik for doing what they do best and that's making sure things happen. I'ma turn the mic to James right fast."

"Blessings, to my fans, followers, and friends along with everyone else out tonight. We formed this party for Kaleem, a good solid brother that loves his people. So, we're gonna show how to have a party tonight!"

The crowd screamed and shouted for like ten minutes as Kaleem walked up to the mic. "Much love, much love!" he said, looking around at all the people. "Thank you, thank you for coming out tonight. I want everyone to have a ball, if not, let me know and I promise my people will make it right. Before I forget, I want to shout out some Brick City men that made it home from behind the walls, Kariem of Scudder Homes, Marvin Ellis, Malik from Brick Towers, Kason from 7th Avenue, Omar Shabazz, Jabo,

Hassan (Howard St.), Aziz, Samad (West Market), Mr. Man, Hakim Lozpen Mo'ment, Farad and Lil Muham (R.I.P). I want to congratulate Kariem and Omar Poohie for their two new novels; Omar 'The Last Round' a memoir about one of the hardest hitters Newark ever had. And Kariem with his 'Brick City' novels that have everyone begging for more! Shout out to my dudes and women locked down, always respect due to you! One love to Sheek (Lil Bricks), Arbak Prey, Breeze, DuDus (Tivoli Garden) and to the one's that may never touch home, much respect to you!"

'Bass line' Pink Panther started the party off with Aidonia's Jockey, Beenie Man. The crowd wasted no time working on the dance floor, winding those hips and getting their grind on and worked out! The music tickled their ears with its thumping bass lines, making it impossible to stand still. The people on the bikes all revved their bikes making the pipes sound like thunder blending into the music as a mix.

Mike Dixon knew it was show time, Sherri, Pam, Cynthia, and Kareemah (Gwenny) was sure to attend. The Drakeford sisters were fly, but down to earth so everyone loved them. They all wore white body fitting shoulderless jumpsuits that were breathtaking. Mike wore an all white suit and waited for more girls to walk with them inside. The girls went straight to the dance floor surrounding Mike.

Zeep, zeep, was the sound of Queen's phone going off. "Hello," she answered.

"Hi, baby!" Kaleem yelled, trying to cover the music enough to hear. "Where are you?"

"I'm coming in now."

"What do you have on?"

"Almost nothing." she lied.

"What!"

"I'll find you, Mr. Kaleem."

"Ok." They hung up.

Queen had on some practical white pants with a lace see through top showing her black Victoria Secret bra, allowing her girls to stand firm and a pair of open toe white sandals.

The Jamaican DJ Fire Links played Barrington Levy's 'On the Telephone'. Everybody was rocking! A Jamaican guy spotted Queen and began dancing with her. Working her hips as though she was from the Islands. All smiles came upon the man's face! A second guy joined the fun. Still, she held her ground on the dance floor and was having fun.

Kaleem overheard a guy at the bar ask his partner, "Who is dude Kaleem anyway?"

Kaleem injected. "He is just a nobody that knows somebody that loves everybody!"

The two men looked at each other in confusion and kept drinking. The videographer zoomed in putting Kaleem on all four projectors. Tony started spinning the music with Stevie Wonder's 'All I do' blowing through the speakers.

Ta'Rod spots Kaleem as they meet on the dance floor around his home girls from the projects. They both greeted each other. Queen saw Kaleem dancing and told the two guys she was dancing with thank you. She noticed her panties were wet and made her way to Kaleem.

"This atmosphere is jumping!" Sabrina said to Monica. Having known Kaleem for years, they were sure to make this event.

Tattooed covered waitresses, painted waitresses, and waitresses in sexy underwear covered the party handing out the champagne. Men in swimming trunks walked around breathing fire. The ladies loved looking and feeling on their carved bodies. The place bubbling with excitement.

"Wow, this is amazing, I'm loving this turn-up!" Kaleem thought.

"Hi, Kaleem." Queen hugged him waiting to see if he wanted to kiss her in front of everyone.

Sure enough, he tongued her down right where they stood. "Where have you been?" he asked.

"Working two Jamaican guys on the dance floor."

"Oh yeah, so are your panties wet?"

"Soaked!" she said with a horny smirk on her face.

"Just know whose gonna do the rest of the job!" he added like a boss.

"Of course, you daddy!" she replied with a smile.

"Let's dance. Ms. Wet Panties!" they both laughed and it was on, their bodies were rocking to the music.

Queen spots her boss Stacey from the corner of her eye. *"OMG, not the devil tonight! I wish she would get run over by a truck."* she thought.

"That's not nice." said the voice in Queen's head.

"You're right, forgive me, but I can't stand her."

Stacey made eye contact with Queen...

"Hey, ain't that your supervisor that be giving you hell at work?" Pat asked.

Queen nodded her head still dancing.

"She bet not come out of her neck wrong or I'ma drag her ass!" Pat told her.

Stacey and her friend Thelma got some champagne from a muscular pecan complexion waiter. Thelma worked at the VA Hospital and was a mouth watering brown superstar. After flirting for a few, the girls were joined by two guys from Myrtle Beach and started dancing with them.

"Yo, mon, you see that?" Dellie asked.

"See what?" Strachie inquired.

"Mi saw that guy put something in the gal drink there!"

"You sure, Dellie?"

"Yeah, mi, sure! He has a tube in his right pocket."

"Hold on, rest yourself. Let's watch for a few." Strachie suggested.

This girl, Joy from PA broke the number one rule: Never leave your drink unattended or with someone you just met. The unknown patron slipped a date rape drug called Rohypnol in her drink. After the two men saw Joy instantly sloppy drunk, they sprung into action. Strachie tapped the man on his shoulder and chopped him in the neck, caving in his throat making him fall to the floor. Dellie went into the man's pocket and pulled out a tube of fluid and poured it down the perverts throat. Security came and let's just say, took him some place to work out. The other girls that were with Joy took her to the room.

"I can't stand that thot!" Stacey said, speaking of Queen.

"Who you don't like!" Thelma screamed.

"That bitch!" she said maliciously. "I caught her trying to screw my boyfriend once. I had to beat her ass!" Stacey boasted, lying through her teeth.

"That's some old BS, look how many women's men you screwed."

"We ain't talking about me. I'm talking about her." she answered with attitude.

"Well, I'm just saying, don't look like she's thinking about you tonight. Plus, I ain't missing work to come bail you out of nobodies jail. So, stop trying to contrive deceitful schemes against her, let it go."

It's now five a.m. It seems like no one even left the party yet. Rippa MC got back on the mic, amping up the crowd. "Now, I want to know, are y'all having a good time!" the crowd screamed. "I can't hear you!" The crowd and the pipes from the bikes sounded off with deafening sounds. "Ladies and gents, Kaleem's boys have a toy for him! Please make room as the bikes come through, making a lane!

Once the forty or so bikes formed a lane, a girl in a one piece leather suit, all black, slowly rode a bike covered with towels.

"Uncover it!" said the MC.

"Wow, damn, oh shit! That's bad! What a bike!" were the words from different people out the crowd.

The bad ass pearl, black and purple Hayabusa motorcycle was a monster. Picture a terrifying visage of a Sabertooth tiger ready to bite you from the front headlights. Kaleem loves the bike, happy as he hugs his boys. He sat on it and felt the 1300 cubic inches of pure power between his legs.

He waved for Queen to come over. "Wanna go for a ride?"

"You've been drinking Kaleem!"

"Yeah, and I promise, I'm not talking about the bike."

Queen began to smile, knowing what he was talking about. He left her profiling, sitting on his new bike, while he continued talking and meeting more people. DJ Na'eem played the club banger, Dr. Love, rocking the crowd.

Queen lift up the kickstand, held the clutch in and pushed the start button. She put the bike in first gear, eased off the clutch, and gave the throttle some wrist and began making the big beast burn out doing donuts. The crowd was getting out the way, but amazed at how she handled such a big bike.

"That's what I'm saying!" Pat screamed in excitement, as others gave high-fives in approval.

"Damn, you're full of surprises. You didn't tell me you could ride."

"You didn't ask, daddy. It's the unknown that turns you on!" she winked an eye at him.

DJ Na'eem mixed Beyonce and Jay-Z's 'On the Run'...

Queen and Kaleem danced with their body movements, timing each other. He sang Jay-Z's part to her and she sang Beyonce's part to him. He's an outlaw with an outlaw chick. Being sexy and seductive with each other, they were feeling the song. Kaleem saw himself loving this woman and enjoying her. Sweat dripped from everyone on the dance floor, and the drinks continued to flow at seven in the morning.

"Let's grab some breakfast at IHOP, ride down the TurnPike and escort the Lost Boys to Exit 1 and ride back. Then I can start feeling myself inside of you."

"I bet you can, Mr. Kaleem, and I can feel you stalking the coochie."

"What! Why you say that?"

"That's how delicious it will be to ya, you won't have a choice!"

"Well, I guess you will have to show and prove your work, Ma! I sure want to see if you can back up all that slick talk."

"Your wish is about to come true. Let's go eat and ride so we can get back. I want us to go to my house once we get back if you don't mind."

"You can even drive going down and I'll drive coming back. I never had a girl put me on the back of no bike."

"First time for a lot of things!"

Chapter 15

The ride on the TurnPike was great. Queen showed she could handle all the power of the bike between her legs riding Kaleem. That turned him on even more! He kept a hand in between her legs, keeping her hot box wet and juicy. The Lost Boys said their goodbyes and rode on. Kaleem and Queen switched and now he's driving. It was off to the races again, the bikers wasted no time speeding up the TurnPike. Everyone knew many of the bikers wouldn't stop if the police came behind them. Most of the time the cops would not chase the bikers anyway because of their high speeds.

Kaleem had some work to do. They agreed to go to Queen's place instead of a hotel…

The day is beautiful, filled with the sunshine, birds singing, and fumes of old cars in the air. Finally, it's about to go down! Kaleem bust a left turn on Montrose St, and drove into Queen's driveway, pulling his bike behind the house, adding extra security. He admired the quiet atmosphere of where she lived. Queen could feel her body juices as she got off the motorcycle. Thinking of all she would do to him and the question she wanted to ask him. They both went inside.

"First thing, first." she thought as she took a deep breath and fixed both of them a drink.

"This is a nice place, Queen. How long have you been here?"

"I've been here for four years now. I like this spot, not too much of anything goes on up here. Plus, I'm planning on going to Seton Hall, which is a few blocks away."

"I appreciate the antique wood and look. By the way, does your television work?"

She gasped for air. "What!"

"Naw, I'm just joking. Can I check out the News?"

"Sure, baby, there's the remote."

Queen was preparing for a wonderful ordeal. She turned on the shower to get the bathroom steamy and hot. Her nookie was throbbing like a heartbeat. She walked into her bedroom admiring her king size bed, thinking, it will get some real action now, not just her pleasing herself. She pulled her duffle bag filled with items from the sex store and Angel's Erotic Solution. She put on a porn DVD, 'In the Bedroom' by Dane Jones because of its sensually explicit creative erotica was filled with teasing and straight hardcore sex!

"Kaleem, I wanted to ask you something."

"What is it, beautiful?"

"What is your goal in making love to me? I mean, am I some kind of trophy or something to you?"

"Queen, I have to feel a connection to you in order to be turned on to make love to you. Anybody can screw and that's a cheap trick. Now, don't get me wrong, a guy can be a cheap trick too. I feel a connection with you for what it's worth, that has me feeling I have emotionally bonded with you, making love to your mind, and led my heart to want your body and soul."

"Wow, I am feeling all of that answer. Now, one more thing, are you into S&M?"

"What the hell is that?"

"It's dominants and submissive's, BDSN… Bondage, discipline/dominance, submission/sadism, masochism, and aficionados."

"As long as none of that means putting anything in my ass!" they both began to laugh. He continued. "Queen, I'm down with everything else that will make this a mind blowing experience for the both of us. The bottom line is, I will make love to you, I will suck you dry, and I will fill every opening in your body. I will give you the most ferocious pain you could endure!"

"I'm sold, I'll take it! I mean you." She emptied her sex toys out her bag onto her bed. Whips, handcuffs, oils, gold balls on a rope, vibrators, finger bangers, leather mask, spikes, straps, gloves with claws, lotions, and a paddle; she had it all!

"Damn, you're ready for a war!" Kaleem joked, but quickly came out of his clothes, and began stroking himself as she watched.

She licked her lips, which turned him on even more. "C'mon," she told him, leading the way into the steamy bathroom.

She made it clear that sexual aggression sultry hot blazing sex is what she wanted the most. They entered the shower allowing the hot water to penetrate their bodies. Queen puts her Dove body wash on her sponge and began to wash her man's body down. Rubbing their bodies together, he lathered her neck, massaging her breast. He slowly cruised between her legs, sliding the sponge up and down her hot box, he knew this would get her blood pumping. She turned her back to him and pressed her booty against his hardened penis. He continued to fondle her breast and coochie. After an hour of shower four-play, they rinsed off and got out. Queen grabbed two towels—

"You won't be needing one," Kaleem told her.

"Why?"

He began blowing from her ear to her neck. The water drops connect to each other as the excitement pleased seeing the water run down her smooth curvy body. Once at her waist, and then between her legs. She admired and was amazed by the blow drying technique, but was she ready for bedroom action. She stopped him and put on a sexy beige and blue lace thong set. They knew that communicating about sex is the key to satisfaction.

They went into the bedroom and she passed Kaleem the bottle of hot oil. He began massaging her neck, relieving her tension, trying to bring her to a calm state of mind. While caressing both her breast, he began squeezing, sucking, kissing, and licking her hardened nipples. Frantically moaning louder and louder, she knew he would know he was doing well. He knows the body has five million touch receptors, and he wanted to touch every one of hers. He put oil on her feet, oiling them down firmly. She kept her weekly pedicure appointment so he had no problem being a foot fetishism, her toes were sucked and kissed vigorously. Both their brains were flooded with chemicals to enhance their bonding. Rubbing the oil on her legs, he could feel the hot steam being released from her body. Using only his lips, he removed her thong. He gently rubs around her clitoris, pressing lightly on her labia. Her skin began to swell, he continued stroking her G-spot. He then placed his face in between her legs, pressing his top lip where the labia separates, and his bottom lip right above the opening. He circled her clitoris with his tongue while applying pressure with his mouth and face.

She started grinding her hot box into his face. He stimulated the inner and outer labia. She bit down on her bottom lip. "Aww, ooh, oh, yeah!" She became crazy enthusiastic when she reached the highest peak from the boast of the blood flow to her genitals and the high dopamine level in her brain. "Yes, right there! Keep doing it, yes!" He was right on the mound of her clitoris, he refuses to let her explode yet. He knew not to rush and that her uterus is a powerful player. He stopped to open a tube of lubricant cream that gave a warm and tingling sensual sensation. She moaned in anguish and clutched her lips. "Don't stop daddy, don't stop!" she begged and moaned. "Yes, um, aww!" Moving her head from side to side. She lifted her right breast up to her lips and began sucking her hardened nipple. The excitement turned Kaleem on. He worked his way to the other nipple driving her insane. He slid back down to her steamy hot juicy box and kissed her all around that area. She took both her hands and massaged his shoulders and head. Moaning and groaning in ecstasy from the great sensation she was encountering. "Ooh, ooh, umm, yes, baby, yes! Daddy!"

"Yes, mommy," he replied.

"Why are you doing this to me?"

"Giving you all you've been missing!"

He knew he was all in at this point, teasing the entrance to her vagina. He slipped his finger into the tight opening, found her G-spot, and rubbed on it while sucking on her clit...

"You're making me cum!" she screams in ecstasy. Kaleem could feel her body tense up as her fingernails ripped into the flesh of his bare back! "Uh, uh, oh God, yes, daddy!" She tried to push his head off her clit, but he fought to keep sucking it to the very last second. She did not have to posit whether he knew how to please her. The way he treated her kitty, sucking, licking, biting, and kissing it, he should have been a doctor, operating the way he did.

Kaleem finally came up for air, revealing the juice from her body that gave him a facial. The air dried the secretion upon his face. She pulled his face down for more!

Queen knew she would be unrestrained in her expose with Kaleem. After several minutes she spoke. "Hold on," she begged. "Oh my God, let me catch my breath!" As she put on her leather face mask connected to a four-inch collar that came down and wrapped around her breast, coming down around her hips with four separate straps for her wrist and ankles. Kaleem looked on in suspense anticipating what is about to happen! She sat up on the bed and cuffed her legs to the solid oak bed post. "Now, lock my wrist to the top post. Take the whip and beat me!"

"What!"

"Take the whip and beat my ass daddy, I've been a bad girl!" she begged. Slap! Slap! Slapping sounds as the leather landed on her skin. "Harder!" she demanded. "Harder!" Slap! Slap! Slap! Slap! "That's all you got damn-it!" Slap! Slap! Slap! Slap! He spanked her until his arms were tired. She enjoyed the vitality of how she could handle pain. Queen knew the way she was strapped to her bed, Kaleem would be thirsty to hit all her pleasure spots. Queen was a certified freak in the sheets.

"Get that We-Vibrator." she insisted. "I want us to use it. The vibrator is a designed sex toy for both our pleasure," she told him.

He put one side into her vagina. It has a vibrating motor that Kaleem will feel on his penis. Then there is a vibrating motor on the outside that will be massaging her clitoris. "Have you used it yet?" he asked her.

"No, it's brand new." She blushed.

She could see the large vein that ran down the shaft of his hardwood. Her juicy coochie made him want to be covered with it on his manhood. He knew the outcome would be a mind blowing experience. "Put it inside of me!" she pleaded.

"I love the way you beg for me to put it inside."

"Please, baby, do it!" she begged, hungry for it.

Just as he entered her he stopped at the frenulum, right where the shaft and head meet, it was indeed tight the way he imagined.

She tightened up as she felt the head of his penis penetrate her opening. Her lower ab muscles made her lip grip him even harder. *"Damn, Kaleem!"* she thought, trying to prevent any premature ejaculation. "Oh my God, take the pussy, daddy! It's yours, daddy! I told you it was tight, give it to me... Yes, yes!" she screamed. The We-Vibe had him very intense as he began pumping her with short strokes until he forced himself to the bottom of her tunnel. "Aww, aww!" she screamed, crying in pleasure. "I can feel you in my stomach, oh my God. You like it?"

"I love this shit!" he answered soaking in her wetness. His testicles slapping against her ass, they both turned on!

Her juices ran down the crack of her butt cheeks onto the sheets. He inserted his finger into her rectum timing both actions at the same time. Kaleem looked in the mirror and felt like a porn star, giving himself an award for the way he was pleasing her. He knew she was about to make him scream, ready to explode! He began hitting deeper and harder inside of her as she continued to scream out in pleasure. "Ooh, fuck me, ooh yes, yes, damn it!" He knew there was no holding back, trying to suppress the more than 1,000 motile sperms that men make every second compared to a woman's monthly egg. She kept throwing, staying in rhythm. Surging up and down her spine, her cerebellum tells her to embrace the oncoming orgasm.

"You coming, mommy?"

"Yes, yes, choke me!" she begged.

"You're making this dick cum, take it!" With both hands around her neck, choking her, giving her what she wanted and asked for; vertigo in her brain encountered turned her on. He was still inside of her while they lay in silence.

Not knowing that Queen was unconscious for a few, she came back and told him to untie her. She gasped for air, getting herself together.

"Damn, ma, you trying to kill me?"

"Are you saying, you can't hang?"

"Hell, naw, I didn't say that. You felt what I'm hitting with."

"What?"

"Yeah, you'll get the rest of your grade after we finish."

She began sucking on his chest and then his nipples. His manhood raised up and she mounts him and begins to ride it. Rotating her hips in a circular and up and down motion, she dug her long nails into his chest, making him bleed.

"How does this coochie feel?"

"Keep working it, don't stop!" he responded, enjoying the moment. He placed both his hands on her hips, pulling her down even harder on his manhood.

"Why are you fucking me like this?" she asked with a seductive look. "Uh, uh."

"I want you to always want this, and I want this coochie to be mine. I'm about to cum!"

She pulled him out of her and begun sucking him vigorously. Even though she had not had sex, she would practice giving a blowjob on bananas. She also watched her share of porn. Placing his testicles in her mouth, she stroked his shaft back and forth. "Ooh, aw, oh, damn!" he moaned. As she licked his inner thigh and blowing on his testicles. He could feel the breeze on his ass making him tense up. She knew she made his toes curl at this point. She moved her hair out the way and played with his testicles like she was on a handball court. "Oh, shit! Ooh, ah!" he yelled as he pushed out the thick white semen. She did not waste one drop. He couldn't take it anymore, begging her to get off his now sensitive manhood.

The mind blowing love making / hard-core sex had Kaleem done! The breathtaking chemistry soared to heights like never before. Love is the most intoxicating, powerful drug there is, and they both enjoyed the experience. After talking about how they enjoyed each other, they fell asleep.

***

Six o'clock the next morning…

Kaleem was the first to wake up. Queen slept on her stomach. He grabbed the essential oils off her nightstand, the organic pink grapefruit scent, and firmly gripped her body with his strong firm hands moving all over her soft body. He finished oiling her down and placed the hot stones on her back. She half asleep, loving the feeling. He slid her Liberator up under her stomach, hoisting her booty in the air, he spread her legs open and began to eat breakfast. Her juices seemed to come harder and faster in more volume than all of yesterday. Flowing more like a river, she was fully awake now having multiple orgasms. She exploded all over his face, causing him to retreat. He removed the hot-rocks and flipped her over and put her legs on his shoulders.

"No," she whispered, knowing she wanted to feel the pain. Looking at her facial expression, he placed his manhood inside of her. "Ooh, ooh, ooh." she moaned. Bracing her arms on the bed, as he gave her long hard strokes. "Deeper, deeper!" She wanted to show him she was a trooper on the playing field. "I'm getting a cramp in my leg" she pleaded. Kaleem never stops pumping and puts his hands around her shoulders, finding the right pressure hitting her spot. They both came at the same time. "This shit is unreal," she said as the alarm clock goes off again after an hour now, and she hasn't been paying it any attention. "Oh my God!" she had forgotten all about work, and she was late. "I have to get to work, you can stay as long as you like, we can even go for two days next time," she said with a smile.

"That sounds like a plan. Let's see how you feel when you get off. I'll have your car dropped off to your job." He looked at her as her naked body disappeared into the bathroom. He thought about how good the sex was. *"Fifty Shades of Grey never saw us in action!"*

Both felt like heaven came to earth. The mind is a powerful force. It can enslave you or empower you. It plunged them into heights of ecstasy from stupendous love making. Queen had no choice but to force herself into work. Not wanting to give Stacey any energy to fire her.

Kaleem drove Queen's car to the hospital and left the keys with security as she requested. After catching a cab to pick up his Honda Accord, he went to the barber shop to check on a few guys while getting a fresh line-up.

Loving Brick City's beautiful women that never stopped showing how powerful God is in creating such a gift to men. Not to forget that pretty face and an ugly and wicked heart is toxic! There is nothing like these Jersey girls that go hard for their city.

Chapter 16

"Hey, Omar Smiley, how is that truck?" asked Kaleem.

"You know I been wanting to get this SRT Jeep Grand Cherokee, it got some power too... A 5.7 Hemi V-8 motor."

"Damn, O, when can I test drive it?"

"Here you go!" Omar passed Kaleem the keys.

"That's what's up. I Ain't doing much tonight, gonna have a few drinks and call it a night. I love the way that black paint looks on your truck, man."

"Word, Kaleem, you know we keep it real with each other."

"Here are the keys to my Honda. I already got my hair cut so I'ma bounce."

"Ok, that's what's up. Call me tomorrow," said Omar.

"That's peace!" They shook hands and departed.

Driving up Springfield Avenue, Kaleem spotted the 43rd Street Café and decided to stop for a few drinks. This spot used to be off the hook; now under new management, you can go there and have a good time. Kaleem's memory played over and over the action pack encounter he shared with Queen. It started to rain as he parked the truck. He had a short run to the front door of the café.

"Hi, you're a new face." greeted Dionne, the beautiful barmaid. She was brown skin, long black beautiful hair, and thick hips for days.

"Yeah, I don't get out much." he replied.

"What can I get you? Are you married?"

"Damn," he said with a smile. "For the first question, I'll have a double of Johnny Walker Black, no ice, and a Bud Light. For the second question, the answer is, no."

"Your gonna need more than that after sleeping with that girl last night." Mr. Devil said.

"Who asked you for your opinion." Kaleem shot back.

"Hell, you could have asked me to put the gun to your head, so you could kill yourself. You won't suffer long." the Devil added.

"I'm ready for whatever, I gave my life to her."

"You're not lying about that." the Devil Agreed.

"Whatever God Does is For the Best." Kaleem thought.

"So you even talk to yourself, huh?" asked Dionne.

Laughing, "No, no, my bad, how much?"

"Fifty, and that's with my ten dollar tip."

"I see you been doing this a while," Kaleem told her.

"Not too long."

Just then another lady walked up to the counter. "Hello, I'm Cookie, the manager. She isn't asking for tips, is she?"

"Hello, naw, she's straight."

Cookie has style and class, looking like a ray of sunshine. Seeing the large rock on her finger, Kaleem knew someone locked her down, showing she was off limits. "Well, enjoy your drink." she said with a smile, softly rolling her hips walking away with her Newark swag.

"Damn." he thought after taking a second look. He is riding on a cloud from feeling his drinks right now, thinking about all he's up against, trying to put things in order. He drank down his beer, placed a twenty dollar tip, and headed for Omar's Jeep. He wanted to ride over to Paterson to holler at his brother Chris since he hasn't seen him. Chris is a weight trainer at Club Metro USA in Paterson, these guys go hard! On the way, he couldn't help but think about Queen, the heart pounding, back aching, eye rolling, hair slinging, licking, sucking, and good hot coochie; delicious type of sex.

***

Driving back down Springfield Avenue, he gets on Garden State Parkway, northbound. In his zone from the drinks, he fails to see the black mustang with black tinted windows lurking behind him. Nodding his head to the sounds of Method Man and Mary J. Blige's 'All I Need', admiring how nice Omar's SRT handled in the rain, Kaleem was sure to cop one for himself. He thought about buying a house for Queen and giving her the best she could imagine... *"A few kids, yeah, like two boys, maybe two girls, or how about a boy and a girl."* Either way, he would enjoy making them. *"Gotta call moms!"*

He reached for his phone to call his mother Fatisha...

"Hello," the soft voice answered.

"Hi, Ma, did I wake you?"

"Hey, baby, I thought about you an hour ago."

"Oh yeah, about what?"

"About how much I miss and love my son. I want you to be careful. Had a vision someone was shooting at you."

"Damn!" he thought. He thought about him and Ta'Rod at the restaurant.

"Ma, don't worry yourself. You look at too much television."

"When are you coming to see me, son?"

"Soon, ma, I have been chilling with your old nurse, Queen. You remember her?"

"Yes, the sweet young lady that took care of me."

The mustang followed patiently, not trying to be noticed.

"Hold on, ma." Both vehicles paid the toll and jumped on Interstate 280. "Yeah, ma, we will be coming down in a few weeks."

The exit for downtown Newark was coming up in two miles. The passenger's side window came down as it pulled up on the Jeep... Kaleem floored the gas pedal.

Fatisha dropped her phone as she heard the gunshots and her son yell the words "oh shit!"

She stared at the phone briefly before yelling his name through the phone. "Kaleem! No, no! Lord, no, not my baby!"

The Jeep hit the cement wall and flipped over once. Kaleem felt the burning sensation on his left side. Everything was thrown all around the truck. He felt around for his gun that fell from his waist. He found his gun! He knew that he couldn't wait inside the truck to be killed, so he climbed out the broken windshield after kicking the rest of the glass out. He could feel his strength leaving. With so many faces flashing through his mind, he doesn't know if this would be the night he'd die. He figured, whoever shooting at him wouldn't hesitate on finishing their job of killing him. If not revenge would be his! *"Damn,"* he said after seeing how his blood now colored his jeans. His eyes were getting lower and lower. The rain still coming down even harder now. He could hear the footsteps from boots getting closer and closer. Dressed in all black and a black face mask, the gunman looked inside the truck and then walked towards the side of the truck, and Kaleem let off one shot at the dark shadow, hitting him in the shoulder. Firing twice more, Kaleem hit nothing. The gunman fired into the ground before falling to the ground. The two men's blood began to paint the wet pavement.

The sounds of sirens were getting closer. Cars pulled over to the sides of the highway to see if they could help. Kaleem fell unconscious... The medical squad arrived first, followed by the Newark Police squad cars. They began taking statements along with taking pictures of the scene. People were telling the police that is was a road rage shooting, lying but what the hell. Both men were transported and under police custody while being treated at the University Hospital.

***

Queen arrived to work the next morning and looked over the charts with the names and conditions of all the patients. Cheryl and Gale are nurses that worked the night shift; they filled Queen in on the action with the two guys that shot each other. After listening to the ladies, Queen walked down the corridor to learn more information about the gossip. She spoke to the officer outside the room and went inside the room.

"Aw, another young man involved in a shooting. When will it ever stop? He looks so innocent." Blaame was still heavily sedated from all the medication he was given to ease the pain.

"Is he ok?" the officer asked, just trying to make conversation with Queen.

"Yes, he will be ok." she replied.

"Once you get finished checking all your patients out, how about you and me grab something to eat."

"Thanks, but, no thanks. I'm on a diet."

"Don't look like you need no diet to me." he replied with a horny smirk on his face.

She walked straight past him without saying another word and went into her next patient room. The clock of the world seemed to stop, her feet seemed to be stuck to the floor, and her heart raced upward once she laid eyes on Kaleem. "Kaleem, Kaleem, Kaleem," she whispered. He could only hear her voice, but couldn't respond. "Oh, God, please take care of Kaleem, please." She rubbed his face with the palm of her hand. She left the room to get herself together. *"Pull yourself together."* she thought to herself. Surely not wanting Stacey to find out that it's Kaleem. She would check on him throughout the day. Kaleem stayed unconscious… Family and friends were calling, but no one was allowed to see him.

Pat went directly up to the hospital as soon as she got the news. She called her sister, Fatisha to let her know that her son would be alright. A mother's intuition will always connect with her child.

Queen's shift had ended. It was time for her to go home and rest for the next day.

***

The next day at the hospital…

"Welcome back, Kaleem," said Dr. Syrkin. "We will be monitoring you for the next two days, and then you will have to deal with the charges they have on both of you guys."

"The both of us?" Kaleem asked puzzled.

"Yeah, your buddy next door is healing also." the Dr. stated sarcastically. "I'll be back in a few hours," he told him as he made his way out the room.

"Right next door!" Kaleem thought to himself.

"Yo, son, we got to get that fool. He tried to do us, son!" the Devil said.

"Chill, just chill, let me think this thing out. I got to get pass that police that's on guard."

"That's small stuff, we got to flatline this dude before he tries us again." The Devil kept the fuel on the flame.

"I promise it won't be the next time," Kaleem mumbled.

***

Two days had past and Blaame was ready to make another move on Kaleem. He thought about how the day shift officer Dennis enjoyed flirting with the women. He would be instrumental in making his move. He hated the fact Kaleem was still alive!

"Good morning, how are you today, beautiful." Officer Dennis spoke to Stacey as she went into Blaame's room.

"Good morning, Officer Dennis, I haven't seen you in a while." she replied.

"Yeah, I've been on night shift for a while. I had to get off that, I had no free time at all. Now we can go out."

"Only if you promise to bring your handcuffs." she told him looking thirsty.

"Morning,"Queen spoke as she walked in Blaame's room to fill out his charts.

"Good morning," Officer Dennis replied, looking hungry. As always, Stacey said nothing and continued what she was doing. Queen knew speaking to Stacey got under her skin.

Blaame had the night nurse to disconnect the morphine they gave him for pain. He didn't want to be drugged up, so he could make his move on Kaleem.

"Excuse me, do you mind finishing his vitals so you can get from around me," she told Queen momentarily while rolling her eyes. This was fine with Queen wanting to get away to see Kaleem anyway.

"How do you feel, Mr. Blaame?" Stacey asked.

"Ready to go home." he replied.

"Well, partner, I hate to inform you, but you're going to jail. You don't want to go home out there shooting people."

"Mind your business, lady, you don't know me! Nosey people get it too."

"Give the lady some respect." the cop said.

"What, I only see one lady in here, this other trick needs to leave me alone," Blaame added.

"Take the handcuffs off his right arm so I can get some blood." said Stacey.

"Sure, anything you need just let me know." Dennis licked his lips as he walked to the bed to remove the cuffs. He stood next to Stacey by the bed as she prepared to draw Blaame's blood.

Blaame saw Dennis has sex on his mind, and how he stood so close to his bed, so he made his move, snatching his gun from his holster. The officer reached for his gun, but was too slow; Blaame was now in control of the situation. "Now that I have everyone's attention, move to the corner of the room!" Both women frantically did as told. "Mr. Police, this ain't for you, so don't try to be a hero today!"

"Please, please, don't hurt anyone. Why are you so angry?" Queen asked.

"I'm mad because Kaleem killed my father!"

"What?" Queen replied.

"Yeah, he was shot at a basketball game at Branch Brook Park, four years ago. I want to kill the guy that killed my dad! I grew up without a father, even though he was never around, he was still my father. Then you got this stuck up ass thot," referring to Stacey. "Treating me like shit just because I'm getting locked up! Your mind is slow, now what room is Kaleem in?" he demanded as the room stood still as the darkness in the night. "I'm not joking!" He pointed the gun at Stacey and fired one shot at her.

Officer Dennis made his move and lunged forward, knocking over hospital equipment. He wrestled with Blaame for the gun. Another shot went off going into the floor. The officer twists Blaame's arm, causing the gun to fall to the floor, and afraid to let him go.

Kaleem came through the door after he comprehended what was happening. He ran over and picked the gun up off the floor...

"Kaleem!" Queen screams.

Kaleem looked up and saw that Queen had been shot in her shoulder. He gave the gun to the officer and went to her. She now realized that she had been shot and tried to hold it together.

While looking into each other's eyes... "You need to get back in your room," Queen told him, smiling as she felt the burning pain.

He moved the hair from out her face. "What happened?"

"I'm sorry, Queen, please forgive me," Stacey said and continued. "She saved my life! She pulled me down out of the way and the bullet hit her."

Three other officers came in and helped control the situation...

"Hurry, hurry, get her to the bed!" Dr. Sirkin said. He was specialized in gunshot wounds.

Stacey cut open Queen's blouse to see where they needed to stop the bleeding from. Everyone rushed into action getting her to the operating room. Kaleem was in a daze, not believing what had just happened. He just wanted for Queen to be ok.

"Whatever God Does is For the Best!"

"Hell no!" Kaleem thought. *"Not in this situation. I hate you, God! Why are you taking us through this if you are who you say you are?"*

"My child, who are you to question me? I made you, you didn't make me!"

"Dr. Sirkin, she has lost two pints of blood." a nurse told him.

"Ok, what's her blood type?" he asked.

"B-positive, and she is infected with AIDS." the nurse added.

"Well, match her plasma up and get it up here fast!" he demanded.

"No, no, don't!" Stacey yelled crying. "Get her B-positive plasma, she doesn't have AIDS."

"Nurse, give me that chart. Dr. Stacey, what are you talking about? It says right here in red ink, AIDS. What the hell is going on? I don't have time to waste, you need to let me know something now!" he yelled furiously.

"I switched her charts with a person with full blown AIDS years ago when I worked in the plasma bank."

"What, are you serious? If so, you get the hell out of my sight!"

Everyone in the room looked in amazement.

The doctor continued attending to Queen. "The bullet went straight through without touching anything," he said to the staff that was helping. "Get me a blood sample and get me some blood up here for her, right now!"

"Now that Stacey admitted and saying what she said about Queen is B-positive and not infected with AIDS, she will be brought up on charges for doing such thing. This is an outrage!" stated Dr. Rell.

Stacey couldn't believe Queen saved her after all she put her through. Stacey played over in her mind, all the things that could happen now that the truth was out...

You never know who you may need help from in life. No one can live in this world alone.

Chapter 17

"Never in my twenty years in the medical field, have I ever seen anyone with a heart as black as yours! How could you torture someone's life like that? Get out of here, now!" he said and demanded angrily. "You will never work in any medical field again!" Dr. Sirkin told her.

Frantically, Stacey ran out the room. An officer was told to follow her to make sure she left the hospital. Everyone was in shock, that she would stoop so low as to do such horrible thing. Just because she didn't like Queen and was so heinous.

For the next three hours, Queen endured surgery. Test after test, finally, she was stable and breathing on her own. Still drowsy from the MEDs, she thought of her trying to save Stacey from being shot. Feeling the pain, not knowing she would be the one who got shot. She recalled the burning sensation and her body sweating with blood, and then she recurred the heart pounding, mind blowing, chilling, juicy, felt so good, voluptuous, hot sex she and Kaleem encountered. Being injected with such passion, the kind of love that makes a woman yearn for in her man. The I get wet just thinking of him kind of man. Truly astonishing kind of man!

Both Blaame and Kaleem were about to be transported to the Green Monster (Essex County Jail).

"Detective Green, let me holler at you for a minute."

"Yeah, Kaleem, what's up?"

"Can I just see her face before I go?"

"I guess I can handle that, after all, you did help save some lives today!" The three officers and Detective Green walked Kaleem to Queen's room.

Even in her pain, Queen still had a glow on her face, maybe because she was thinking of Kaleem.

"Her vitals are good, and she is doing well." the doctor said attempting to ease Kaleem's pain. "Thanks to you, this didn't become worse."

"Detective, I want to give her my necklace, it's inside my property bag."

He pulled out a half-inch box diamond cut rope, 18 karat gold chain, with an iced out letter 'K'. Green pulled the chain out and gave it to the doctor. He then placed it on her neck.

"Whatever God Does is For the Best," Kaleem whispered to her.

"Let's go, Kaleem!" Green demanded.

***

Detective Green broke the silence on the ride to the county. "You seem to care a lot about that nurse back there. I hope things work out for you, Kaleem. You have a good heart, and the streets say you can become a storm also!"

Kaleem could care less about what was being said, he was thinking of Queen.

"One thing an old man told me that would always let me know where I stand in life is... 'Boys are born, men are made, boys take, men give, boys quit, men fight, boys leave their families, and men take care of their families.'"

Pulling up to the Green Monster, the detective turned and told Kaleem, "One thing for sure, if you stay prayed up, you will be fine. Good luck!"

"Thanks." They walked inside...

***

Inez called Pat and told her to meet her at the hospital. Applesauzz and Cookie had already arrived.

"My baby!" Inez screams as the tears rolled down her chiseled Indian looking face. There were two nurses on call that knew Inez, they explained what happened to Queen, including what Stacey did to her. Inez was shocked by what she was told. "Whatever God Does is For the Best!" she continued to pray. "God, I thank you for keeping my daughter safe and in your care. Please forgive both of the guys who didn't mean to shoot her and Stacey since she doesn't understand that her peace will only come from GOD. Thank you for the staff, which works so hard daily saving lives, they are heroes. I thank you for the love of Queen's girlfriends that support her through all she's gone through. Please keep your angels over Kaleem, Amen!"

"Amen!" the girls repeated.

***

The next day, about the dust of the night, Pat and Applesauzz headed over Society Hill to pay Stacey a visit. There was no way Stacey would get away with what she did to their girl. The girls came out to cut Stacey's face up with two razors to remind her what she did to Queen for so many years! Society Hills are brownstones that connect with nicely manicured lawns in a quiet area. They parked on South Orange Avenue and Howard St and then walked inside the community. The black iron rails guided them up the ten stair steps that lead to the front door, which held the address 22B of Stacey's condo.

***

Back at the hospital, Queen regained consciousness. Her moms sat by her side the whole time. The investigators and doctors just explained again, what Stacey did and wanted her to press charges.

Queen gathered her thoughts and began crying.

Inez wiped her tears and said, "Whatever God Does is For the Best! Queen, what God has for you, no one can ever take it away, no matter what you go through in life."

"Is Kaleem ok? Where is he?" Queen asked.

"They took him to the county with the guy that shot you."

"Ma, he didn't even mean to shoot me, he tried to shoot Stacey."

"Excuse me, Ms. Mack, we need you to sign so we can obtain a warrant." said the investigator.

Queen became irate, but stayed focused and began to speak. "That's what we call snitching and that's not an option." Kaleem taught her well. "What she did is irreversible and I will not take her through the pain and heartache she took me through. I refuse to let anything or anyone steal my joy, so no office, I won't sign anything.

"But do you..."

Queen cut him off abruptly, "No, no, no, and please, leave my room!"

"Hallelujah!" Inez injected.

"Ma, I'ma need you to go bail him out. Get my American Express Black card out my bag. Brick City bonding will be picking him up. Queen felt the necklace on her neck and began to smile, *"That's my man."* she thought.

***

The girls knocked on Stacey's door for a while... She never answered.

Stacey regretted the way she agonized Queen. After so long she broke her silence and answered the door. "Who is it?"

"Ho, open the door, and you'll find out!" Pat replied.

Stacey took the top cover from the shoebox that sat right beside her revealing the snub nose 44 magnum. She placed it in her hand and spun the chamber, rotating the hollow point bullets. She pointed the gun, and then took a deep breath and squeezed the trigger...

Boom! The gunshot rang throughout the apartment. Pat and Applesauzz fell at the bottom of the stairs scraping up their knees. Pat helped her up as the two ran towards South Orange Avenue.

"She shot me in my leg!" Applesauzz said hysterically.

"Oh my God! Let me see!" Pat inquired and looked. "Girl, that's where you fell on your knee and it's bleeding!"

"Damn, that shit hurts like a bullet!"

"Shut the hell up, girl! Shit, she either shot through the door or killed herself one," said Pat.

"You think she went out like that?"

"I'm going back to find out, listen." Police sirens were coming closer and closer, so the two girls bounced.

***

"I'll get it done." Inez agreed to sign for Kaleem to get out of jail. "But, I don't like putting my name on stuff."

"Ma!"

"Queen, stop. C'mon, I love him too, I got it covered."

"I love you, mom. Hey, ma, speaking on the girly side of things, he takes me to another world."

"Girl, please, I don't want to hear that juicy stuff. So, he can handle his business?"

"I thought you didn't want to hear it."

"I don't, I just want to know is his father around?"

"Yeah, ma, and a handsome man," Queen told her. they both laughed.

The girls made it back to the hospital. They both agreed to keep quiet. After talking for more than two hours, the Eye Witness News team came on with a 'Special Report'...

"Live from Newark... A female doctor was found shot and killed in her condo apartment in Newark's Society Hill around 7 p.m. Police don't have a motive right now, but witnesses saw two ladies running from the complex this evening."

"What, was that Stacey?" Queen questioned.

Natalie ran into the room and verified that indeed it was Stacey, she had killed herself.

"Oh my God!" Queen replied in shock.

"Queen, we about to be out." said Pat.

They both gave her hugs and kissed her before they left.

"Love y'all, be safe, bye!"

"What are we gonna do?" asked Applesauzz when they walked out the room.

"We ain't gonna do nothing but keep our mouth shut!" Pat demanded.

Queen said a short prayer for Stacey, and then they continued to watch the news...

Other Headline News today... It appears all gangs in Newark has come together and made a truce to stop the violence and killings. They vowed to protect and build up their city. "We come at you live in front of Newark City Hall! We are here with a gang member 40-Cal and Montana. Your gangs felt that things needed to change Newark as well?"

"Yes, I agreed with the rest of the guys here. We've been killing each other for way too long. We see they want us to kill off our breed. We will make sure all members finish school and you can't be affiliated until your twenty-one years old." 40-Cal replied.

"Montana, you want to say something?"

"Yeah, see, I'm from New York, but I see my brothers pushing positive energy, fixing up abandoned houses, food banks, and we will enforce when anyone breaks the codes of, All Lives Matter! I also want to shout out all my homies locked down fighting for their freedom in the crooked injustice system of South Carolina. It's time for the feds to take county by county starting with Horry County around the Myrtle Beach area!"

"Thank you, two men. For more information on this, please check out our website news7.com, thank you."

Next... Lead found in Newark School systems, How long had this been going on? How many kids has it infected? Angry Newark parents want answers! Parents gathered in front of the board of Education building in Newark. More at eleven tonight.

Next... Newark police had more than three hundred guns and rifles turned in by an unnamed source. This was a major help to the people of Newark. Interview with Newark's Chief of Police at eleven tonight.

Next... man convicted after serving sixteen years for a horrendous murder of his friend... more detail at eleven.

Chapter 18

Kaleem never made it through processing before the bondsman called to let the county jail know they would be to picking him up the very next day. Once he saw the judge he would get a bail.

"Damn." Kaleem thought. *"I want to see, Queen. She was shot because of me. It's all my fault, this is what I was trying to explain to her. But, no, she didn't want to hear any of it. She's a tough chick. Her sex game is like a brawl, she turns into a beast. I got to put her in the top ten porn vixens!"*

"She's got AIDs, you dumb ass!" the Devil injected.

"Ok, well, tell me who on earth is perfect! O, you're telling me, that a person with AIDS or any sickness shouldn't be loved?"

"Listen, kid, you're asking the wrong person, I'm the Devil, I don't have no love for anybody in the world!"

"No shit. Everybody knows that that's the truth. Just so you know, I'm gonna be with her no matter AIDs, HIV, Cancer, no leg, no arm, no coochie... Nah, hold up, let me take that one back!" he laughed. Thinking to himself how good the coochie was, he would put it in a museum.

"Well, you had one, you had them all!"

"That's a lie!" Kaleem responded.

"Don't say I didn't warn you... I'ma keep doing me, destroying families, making people love the streets more than they love their families, breaking up friendships with hatred, greed, envy, and lust. I'm that dude, people love what I do to them. A marriage will never make it if they roll with me. See, most people love what I do for them!"

"I'm straight, Devil, I don't need you, I'm rolling with God! If it ain't about love, it ain't 'bout nothing. I'm going to sleep, leave me alone."

Like clockwork, Kaleem was released at 4 p.m. the next day. After dreaming all night of Queen, he couldn't wait to see her. He thought that he remembered Blaame from a few nights ago, a dude he met at the club with Na'eem and Hakim.

Kaleem walked outside the Green Monster (County Jail)...

"Yo, Kaleem!" Yelled CO-D. A solidly built, brown-skin country brother from South Carolina, with a gold tooth that brightens his smile. He came to Jersey after learning how illegal the judicial system is towards blacks, and whites in South Carolina whom can't afford a good, fair team that don't take your money, and then work for the State. "What's good, my nigga?"

"Chill with that 'N' word, bruh. You know I don't use that word at all."

"That's right, Kaleem, my bad. How you, fam? I ain't seen you in a minute. You need a ride or something?"

"Yes, I need to go to University Hospital on Bergen."

"Shit, Bruh, I almost got locked up last night, myself."

"What happened?" Kaleem inquired.

"I was seeing this chic name Mindy for about two months, right."

"Hold up, don't tell me she was married!"

"Hell, yeah, she told me he was a friend, feel me? So, anyway, ol' girl came with me to my house from the club, spent a night, and went home the next morning. Check it, her husband beats her so bad, she gives him my address. He and four other guys come to my spot and start trying to kick my door in. I'm standing on the other side with both my guns pointing at the door. My door was only being held up by a screw in the hinges of the door. So, I'm praying, telling myself the first face I see I'ma unload every bullet I have. Then all of a sudden one guy told the others, 'Hey, people are coming, we know where he lives, we can catch him later!' Kaleem, just one more kick and I would have been locked up for the rest of my life, 'cause a joker don't know how to take care of home!"

"Damn, bruh, that was wild!"

"You telling me. It's all good, I'ma leave her alone. I could have stayed in Columbia for the craziness!"

"I feel you. I appreciate the ride." They shook hands as Kaleem dropped a twenty dollar bill on the seat and closed the door.

Kaleem walked into Queen's room catching her by surprise. "How are you, my lady?"

A smile came across her face instantly, seeing the man that took her heart. Tears of joy flowed as she cried uncontrollably about all the things she'd been through. She knew she had to tell that she isn't infected.

"Whoa, whoa, whoa, you just took a bullet a few days ago, now you scared 'cause I came to see you." he said smiling.

"I don't want to have to bust you up, who's scared?" She wiped her eyes and then held out her arms for a hug.

Kaleem walked to her bed and gave her a hug. They passionately kissed for a good long minute, while he ran his hands between her thighs. He felt the heat and wetness coming from her body and began rubbing her clitoris. He seemed to promptly get her hot juices flowing like a faucet.

"Please, stop, someone's coming." she begged.

"Yeah, it's you," he claimed as he removed his wet hand from under her gown. He walked into the bathroom just as the doctor checked in on Queen. He informed her that she was being discharged today.

Expressing sympathy for what happened to both women, the doctor admired Queen's virtue. "Your vitals are good. I will have your paperwork completed by the evening."

"Thank you for all your help." she replied.

"Not a problem. It was my pleasure," he told her and then walked out.

Queen could feel Kaleem's vicinity as he cracked open the bathroom door and asked her to come to him. She grabbed her Kimono (Japanese gown) and walked over to the door, telling him she will be released today. He heard nothing she said, taking her hand and pulling her in.

"You're crazy!" she stated after finding, Kaleem had removed all of his clothes. "Wait until we get out of here!"

"Shhh, shhh…" he put his hand over her mouth stopping her from talking. Kissing her on and around her neck, she quietly begged him to stop, while her heartbeat and adrenaline raced from her excitement. He pulled open her Kimono, while his hard manhood pointed directly towards her pleasure zone. He grabbed himself and slid up and down the top surface of her vagina. Feeling the hot wet juice covering all of his meaty head. It was as though he painted the outside of her juice box with his penis. Her body tensed up each time his penis hit her clitoris. Kaleem knew she was producing small orgasms back to back.

This tranquilizing effect made her say. "What are you trying to do to me?"

"Wanting to make you feel me inside of you even when I'm not around you." he said gently. Without protection, he pushed the head of his hardwood inside of her!

"Aww, aww, aww." sounds from her enjoyment softly in his ear. "It feels so damn good." Her hardened nipples enticed him to lift her right breast to suck and blow on it. "Please, put it inside. I want it," she begged breathlessly, whispering in his ear. While massaging his body with her hands, he entered her wet tight vagina. His body determines the stroking making her pump back, building up to exploit and evict the thick white creamy secretion juices that wanted to exit both of their bodies, with both showing endurance to please each other, it was a matter of time. His boldness turned her on. While rubbing her clitoris with the long, deep strokes inside of her, she exploded! Letting go as her body began to shake and tremble. Kaleem realized that she reached her climax, so he pulled himself out of her. He turned her around and bent her over. He *was not* done! Queen balanced herself with one hand on the doorknob and the other, on the sink.

"Do you love…" Kaleem abruptly cut her words off by thrusting all of his penis penetrating inside of her from the back. "It hurts!" she wailed. "Oh God, it hurts! Ooh, ooh, aww! She rotated her waist as if she was a professional pole dancer. Around and around, up and down, while keeping him inside of her hot wet coochie. He pulled her hair back, guiding her. He showed her no compassion as he gripped both sides of her hips and generously dug deeply in and out of her. She bit down on her bottom lip in an attempt to ease her pain and not scream.

"Hey, Queen!" yelled Natalie as she walked into the room. "Come on out that damn bathroom."

"I'm on the toilet!" Of course, she lied.

"Girl, I'm hungry. I got to tell you about my date from last night."

"Shhh, shhh, stop, mmm, mmm…" were the sounds Queen made from Kaleem thrusting inside of her. He was determined to climax and let Natalie know Queen was getting the business right now. So he kept pumping making her ass cheeks slap against his thighs, he gave more enthusiasm and endurance.

Natalie eyes 'bout fell out of her head once she caught what was going on. "Girl, I'm out of here. Handle your business. I'm sorry, I'm out!"

Queen could not respond as she whispered: "Yes, yes, I'm cumming, Kaleem!"

They climaxed at the same exact time. Kaleem stood on his tiptoes making sure every single drop of his fluids came out of his now soft penis.

"Are you trying to kill me, or give me a heart attack." she implied.

"Baby, if dying making love to you like that is gonna kill both of us, we've better be ready."

"You felt so good, I wanna cry. I can't be messing with you like that at my job, a sister got to pay the bills."

"I'll make sure I speak up for you at the union meeting."

"What?"

"I'm just joking, baby!"

The two cleaned themselves up and the doctor brought her release papers.

"I want you to hear this song Beyonce and Jay-Z wrote... Pass me my iPhone, Kaleem."

"Sure. What's the name of it?"

"On The Run." She pressed play on her phone and Bee's voice began to sing...

"Listen to all that she says... I'ma be all that and much, much, more. She spoke enthusiastically. I wanted you to know... Hold up before I tell you, I want to ask you why didn't you ever use a condom?"

"To show you, I'm with you for the long haul, beautiful, no matter what, nothing changes the way you make me feel."

"Wow, you sure have a way with words, sir. Let's go home," she stated.

"Hold up, you said, let's go home? So, I get my own keys," he said playfully.

"Only if you do me like the big bad wolf did Little Red Ridding Hood, and eat me all up!"

"Well, my new name is, Mr. Wolf!" they both laughed.

***

"On the real Kaleem... Well, Stacey admitted that all those years I have been thinking I had AIDS, she changed the blood chart on my DNA when she worked downstairs."

"What! Ain't no damn way!"

Queen began to cry. "Yes, I am healthy... I don't have AIDS!" Tears melted out of Kaleems eyes as well. He felt the joy and pain, hugging her hereafter. "You took me as I am and that really touched my soul. I am in love with you and I want to be with you. I need you in my life, Kaleem!"

"Listen, baby, I'm sorry for all that happened. I'm speechless as to how somebody could do a person such as yourself like that. When I see her I'm gonna slap fire out of her ass!"

"No, Kaleem, she killed herself."

"How, when?"

"After she told everyone, the doctors made her leave the hospital."

"Well, I'm not gonna lie and say I'm sad. I mean, ain't no telling what else she did to people."

"Kaleem, you know I have love for everyone, so I must forgive her if I want to live. Not for her, but for me. I must put that behind me. You're in my life now I have nothing else to lose but everything to gain."

"I got to help you get well. I want to train you on how to protect yourself."

"I know how to protect myself. I took two years of self-defense classes," she said.

"No, beautiful, I mean, how to save your life if someone is trying to kill you. You must learn how to kill. It can be a situation when it's either you or them!"

"Whatever you want to teach me, I'm with you."

"I want your hustle to be tough, a lady in the streets and a freak in the sheets. Your swag is outstanding, I love that in you, Queen."

"So, I think we should move, like, down south Jersey. What you think about that, honey?" she asked.

"I can deal with that," Kaleem answered.

"I will find another job. I don't want to be here anymore!"

"Whatever you want. I will get me a job as well. We can even work together."

"You know how to work?"

"Oh, you got jokes, huh?" he laughed.

"So, are you going to be my doctor?" she inquired.

"I sure am, call me, Dr. Love!"

"As long as you operate like you do, I'ma call you anything you like. Now let's get out of here!"

Kaleem drove Queen's car. When they got to her house, someone broke in and searched her entire place! What were they looking for? Who were they looking for? Kaleem picked up the note on the table that reads...

To be continued

Life is What You Make It

Life is what you make it, though for granted some people take it…

Time is of the essence, but, it only takes a second to waste it…

The same person you were raised with will smoke you like a Jamaican…

So, technically speaking they are foul, I call the flaverent…

Jealousy in their hearts, hatred with such passion…

They wear their emotions on their sleeves and snitching like it's a fashion…

As the story unfolds, jokers lose their morals and codes…

Real gangstas move in silence, but you orally told…

The game ain't the same, no rules, no regulations…

Men with female tendencies, what happened to pride and preservation…

Take ya mind and elevate it, don't be mentally sheltered…

Your mind is in a cage, so you're physically helpless…

Handicapped, to say the least, don't slip these streets a beast…

With cocaine claws, heroin fist, and bullet teeth, the pills you keep dumping will make you weak, while you're sleeping the Devil creeps, idled minds are his play shop…

Just because the whistle blows don't mean the play stops…

Great things come through patients victory is sweet, I can taste it…

You can die for something vacant, but life is what you make it…

My name is Kariem and I approve this positive poem written by, Dishon 'Shizz' Baker, never stop pushing positive energy, my brother, one love!

Get your copy today!
Amazon
BRICKS4Lifepublishing.com
Ebook
Kindle

The Scudder Home Family

Anderson	Howel	Smith
Andrews	Hatchett	Spivey
Adam	Hardin	Suggs
Alexander	Harrison	Scudder
Brown	Hutchinson	Sapp
Bowan	Ingram	Stone
Bradly	Jackson	Williams
Battle	Kearney	Walker
Camacho	Kenney	Wombel
Cotton	Long	
Clark	Lightsey	
Crawford	Lamply	
Castleberry	Mack	
Carter	Marshall	
Cheeseboro	Moore	
Dickey	McKenith	
Dixon	Melton	
Davis	Mance	
Drakeford	Lomax	
Ewards	Little	
Fulton	Myers	
Gillette	Miles	
Green	Perez	
Garner	Phielps	
Goines	Peoples	
Garrett	Phillips	
Grant	Powell	
Howel	River	
Hardin	Robertson	
Hester	Roundtree	
Hampton	Snell	
Hill	Sanders	
Hammans	Sykes	
Harris		

The Author's Interview

1. Tell us why you wrote Brick City?

I once read a quote by Antonie Fuqua, the director of Training
Day, that said. "We all have a story to tell." I wanted to show that
positive change is within anyone. That sometimes we have to go
through things in life, we stumble and pick ourselves back up and
ask ourselves, "What just happened and why?" before we can
really start to understand things, and somewhere in all that turmoil,
we can begin to see that there's a connection between one's own
personal life experiences and the lives of others!

2. What type of readers do you target in your novel?

Anyone that has or knows someone that is struggling with personal
issues. It shows positive change no matter what we go through in
life we can overcome it!

3. Tell us about how you picked your characters?

The plan was to pick people everyone could relate to. That we all
have the power to be kings and Queens!

4. Did you have a lot of support in this project?
Well, yes and no. You see, I stay prayed up and what's for me is
for me! People like to see things with their own eyes, now they
see, and I got to thank all my readers that follow me!

5. What struggles have you encountered?

LOL, funny you ask… I had moved to Horry County, South
Carolina to chill out and retire from the city life. The Lady of
Justice wears a blindfold and the judicial administration, judges
(some), and solicitors (most) will do anything to obtain a
conviction. I was given forty years with no direct evidence in the
form of DNA or fingerprints, with a confidential informant as a
witness who credibility was 'completely' discounted during her

extensive cross-examination. Having found no relief until I reached the South Carolina Supreme Courts, they overturned my conviction after 11 years based on the Judges (Allen Charge) in which the judge's language was coercive. The Supreme Court the added the State's case against me was tenuous at best! Wow! Am I upset with the Jurors? No, I'm not. They didn't expect the solicitor to tell people what to say when they got on the stand. The solicitor is the one who broke the law and oath in which he was hired to uphold. Still, through it all, I have been blessed so, so, much, you wouldn't imagine! By the time you're reading this, I will be out doing what I love and helping people! What they planned to be for bad, in turn, was a blessing, mentally, physically, and financially. I'm from the Brick!

6. What do you think would help our Country Judicial System?

That the dictators, prosecutors, judges, police, and jurors be held liable for their action. Until then, the justice system will never change for the better. With more than two million people incarcerated, they know what's going on but fail to fix the problem. This is one reason so much hate goes towards people of law. Every juror before they take the oath to be a juror, they should be educated on the many wicked acts which occur daily within the justice system across America. A book that can enlighten anyone is, I am Innocent by Jay Robert Nash. This book will teach you more than you could imagine. Another book, The Making of a Slave by Willie Lynch, is just mouth dropping... Ladies, check out Searching For Souls by Mikal Bethea, this is a must have in your life. To the men, Searching For Souls will enlighten you also! Last but not least, Writing On The Wall by Munia Abu-Jamal.

7. Will you write another novel?

Of course I will. I will also be pursuing a movie deal.

The text below is from a reader of Brick City, which we never knew each other until she purchased my novel...

Reader Lisa L: "Thanks so much, I have been dealing with some situations in my life lately. I thought about giving up on some things, but as I read your book, it kept repeating to me, 'Whatever God Does is For the Best!' So I'ma live life to the fullest and not let what was getting me down keep me down. I'ma pick my head up and do like the pencil, see the world with a purpose. You're an inspiration to me. God Bless!

Author Kariem: This is just one of quite a few. This is what makes it all worth while when I can touch the life of someone. That to me is priceless! Thank you so much, Lisa. You are a Queen and have a purpose in life, stand tall, my sister!

We must find truthfulness as our foundation that accepts no imitations. I found this is a fact that can't turn back the words "I Am A Man" that we are quick to say. Is this the truth or just sounds good to say truthfully how can I learn what I've never been taught, this type of lesson can't be bought. Reality said, "It's up to me to be the best I can be." Now, I can see the only thing that holds me back is me. I  will walk the path of many great men, the honor of true men. Integrity, Honor, Responsibility, Respect, Loyalty, and Love. Sore great heights, be the best you can be and implicate your words into action. I did my best today and tomorrow is another day!

Peace, Kariem

R I P UGGIE
Newark New Jersey miss you down here